"Hey, it's okay." Piper stepped backward out of his arms. "It's probably just the wind coupled with some ice on the power lines."

"Maybe it's nothing. But maybe it's something." Benjamin's hand ran down her arm and squeezed hers. "Either way, get behind me and stay close."

Tempting. But no. She'd spent way too long trying to rid herself of the dizzying butterflies that soared through her veins whenever Benjamin was near. She wasn't about to lose her head now. Sure, back on the island last summer she'd thought their relationship was heading somewhere romantically. Right up until he'd taken her out to dinner her last night on the island only to blindside her with the news that he was determined to remain a commitment-free bachelor for the rest of his life.

"Power goes out around here all the time in the winter." She pulled her fingers out of his grip. "It usually comes right back within minutes. But even if it is someone dangerous, I'm going to meet it head-on."

Maggie K. Black is an award-winning journalist and romantic suspense author with an insatiable love of traveling the world. She has lived in the American South, Europe and the Middle East. She now makes her home in Canada with her history teacher husband, their two beautiful girls and a small but mighty dog. Maggie enjoys connecting with her readers at maggiekblack.com.

Books by Maggie K. Black

Love Inspired Suspense

Killer Assignment
Deadline
Silent Hunter
Headline: Murder
Christmas Blackout

Visit the Author Profile page at Harlequin.com.

CHRISTMAS BLACKOUT

MAGGIE K. BLACK

HARLEQUIN® LOVE INSPIRED® SUSPENSE

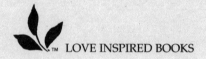 LOVE INSPIRED BOOKS

Recycling programs
for this product may
not exist in your area.

ISBN-13: 978-0-373-44706-0

Christmas Blackout

Copyright © 2015 by Mags Storey

www.Harlequin.com

Printed in U.S.A.

I will lead the blind by ways they have not known, along unfamiliar paths I will guide them; I will turn the darkness into light before them and make the rough places smooth. These are the things I will do; I will not forsake them.
–Isaiah 42:16

ONE

Benjamin Duff gripped the steering wheel with both hands and tried to turn into the skid. It was too late. Pelting sleet and freezing rain had turned the southern Ontario back road into a treacherous mess of slush and ice. The storm had picked up quickly. He'd been just a fraction of a second too late in catching the change of traction from paved road to country lane.

Now his pickup truck was spinning.

Benjamin held on tight as the world flew past the windshield in a blur of gray and white.

Trees. Snow. Sky.

Lord, please keep us safe.

The truck gave a final rotation and came to a stop.

He looked out. Branches, heavy with snow, buffeted against the driver's-side door. The truck was now pointed back the way he'd come, but he'd somehow managed to stay out of the roadside ditch. He rested his forehead on the steering wheel and let out a long breath. "Thank You, God."

The hospital room where he'd spent so many months in traction as a teenager flashed through his mind. It would be sixteen years this February since a terrible snowmobile accident had taken a friend's life and left fifteen-year-old Benjamin with a body so broken that doctors didn't know at first if he'd ever walk again. Since then, he'd built a successful business as an extreme sports instructor and even used the lingering notoriety as a platform to teach thousands of young people about outdoor safety and living life to the fullest.

Now his business was successfully sold. He was just three days away from catching a Christmas night flight to Australia, to pick up the boat he'd saved his entire life for. First he'd embark on a year long sailing voyage for charity. Then he'd use his new boat to start his own Pacific charter service.

Life on the open waters meant that finally he'd be living somewhere he could escape the long shadow the accident had cast over his life.

Yet here, in an instant, he'd been reminded of just how easily everything could be taken away again.

Not that that he'd ever forgotten.

A soft whimper came from the passenger seat.

"I'm sorry, Harry." Benjamin slid one hand into the dog's thick fur. He scratched the young black-and-white husky on the back of the neck, just where the seat belt clipped into his safety harness. "Don't worry. We're almost there. Piper's bed-and-breakfast is only a few minutes away."

I hope.

He eased the truck back onto the road and kept driving. He'd met Piper Lawrence during the summer, when the spunky brunette had walked into his sports shop. Truth be told, they'd barely kept in touch since then and he didn't know her all *that* well. But he knew she had a bed-and-breakfast, on a huge property on the edge of

Lake Erie. While Harry was a pretty good dog he sure wasn't suited for life on a sailboat, so he'd asked Piper if she'd be interested in giving him a new permanent home. She'd said yes.

But the weather forecast was pretty much as bad as the holidays could be. His deep blue eyes glanced at the console clock. It was quarter to four. It was a seven-hour drive from here back to his sister's place on Manitoulin Island, the home he had shared with her. At this rate, he'd be driving well into the night.

"See, dog, Meg and Jack are getting married on Christmas Eve, which is the day after tomorrow." Maybe talking out loud would calm both the husky and himself. "Sounds like your Christmas will be exciting, too. Our friend Piper is hosting a huge Christmas Eve thing."

Our friend Piper. He scratched his trim brown beard. Why did it feel weird to call Piper Lawrence a "friend"? But he couldn't think of a better term to call her. The second to last week of August, he'd just looked up over the counter one day and saw Piper there in the doorway. A mess of tumbling dark hair, plaid shirt worn over jean shorts, sparkling eyes behind huge, round glasses. The dog had charged her instantly, tail wagging. Puppy love at first sight.

She'd had just four days on the island and only been there to escort her aunt. But there'd been this glint in her eyes that told him she could use an adventure. So, he'd done his best to find her one. Together they'd gone hiking, boating, parasailing and waterskiing. Sure seemed like a friendship. Good one, too. But then, when they'd gone out for dinner her last night on the island, somehow everything had gone from comfortable to awkward between them, and he still didn't know why.

"But when it was time to find you a new home, she was the first one I emailed." Benjamin ran one hand through Harry's fur. "Living all by herself, taking care of a bunch of strangers, Piper could use a guard dog, I figured."

He dialed her on his cell phone, which was mounted on the dashboard. The hands-free earpiece was clipped to the corner of his tuque.

"Hello?" Piper's voice filled the car.

Something about her voice always reminded him of salted caramel. Sweet and light on the surface, yet down-to-earth and gritty at the same time.

"Hey. It's me. Benjamin. I'm sorry. I'm running a bit late."

"A bit? I expected you hours ago." Her tone was somewhere between frustrated and worried. Whatever the tension was between them, this probably wouldn't help.

"Yeah, I'm really sorry. Had a lot of goodbyes to get through and you're my last stop—"

"Hang on. The signal's patchy. I'm just carrying some Christmas decorations down to the barn. I was going to wait until after you'd left. But I didn't expect you to be so late and now the storm is getting worse." There was the crunch of footsteps. He heard the sound of a door creaking and the dull sound of stomping. "Now when—"

A loud bang shook the air.

He heard the clatter of her cell phone hitting the floor.

Then the muffled sound of someone screaming.

"Piper? Piper! Hey? You okay?"

The phone went dead.

A shiver shot down his spine. He hit Redial. The call didn't go through.

The dog growled.

"Don't worry. She probably just got startled by something and dropped her phone."

He hoped. He prayed. Eighteen months ago, a serial killer had targeted his sister, Meg. It's what had brought her and her fiancé, Jack, together. Ever since, every unexplained footstep had sounded just a little more ominous.

Benjamin's headlights flickered over a wooden sign for The Downs Bed-and-Breakfast. The house lay straight ahead. A smaller sign advertised Christmas Eve at The Downs and Barn. He followed the arrow and pulled a sharp right and found himself driving down a slope toward the barn where he'd find Piper. "See, we're here."

The truck jolted over uneven ground. The twisting lane dipped even steeper. Wet snow pelted vertically across the windshield like Impressionistic paint strokes. When the trees parted, he spotted a large wooden barn at the bottom of the hill. The frozen surface of Lake Erie spread out behind it. He hit the brakes but the truck kept inching forward slowly. The hill was in desperate need of both plowing and sanding. Even with snow tires it might've been better to wait for Piper at the house.

He tried the phone one more time. Still, no answer.

Below, the barn door opened and someone walked out. Didn't look like Piper. No, this was a big, wide, grizzly bear of a man. The man was dragging something behind him. He hoisted it onto his shoulders, took a few shaky steps across the snow and then dropped it.

Not it. *Her.*

The man was dragging a woman's body out onto the lake.

Benjamin's heart stopped cold.

She started thrashing, flailing and kicking out against her attacker.

Piper!

Piper was fighting for her life down on that ice.

And he was too far away to save her.

Ice smacked hard against Piper Lawrence's body, jolting her into consciousness. She opened her eyes but couldn't see anything. She tried to turn her head and felt the rough sting of burlap on her cheek. Her glasses were gone. Someone had pulled a feed sack over her head. She tried to scream but the string around her neck choked the air in her throat. Her hands were tied together in front of her at the wrists by the very same string now looped around her neck. She could barely move her arms without choking.

Lord, please save me.

A hand grabbed her ankle, pulling her backward. She twisted around, flailing from one side to the other as she tried to wrench her leg from his grasp. He laughed. It was an ugly sound that filled her veins with dread. She kicked back hard and made contact. The man swore and let go.

She dragged herself to her feet. She was running blind. Desperately her fingers pulled at the string around her neck as freezing rain smacked her body.

Disjointed memories filtered through her fear like pieces of a nightmare. She'd walked into the barn carrying a box of decorations. She'd been talking to Benjamin on the phone. Someone in a ski mask had rushed her in the darkness and thrown her against the wall. It was all a blank after that, until the moment he'd dropped her in the snow.

Please, Lord. Help Benjamin realize something's wrong and come looking for me. He's the only person who even knows I'm here.

She could hear her attacker behind her, muttering curses and gasping for breath. She stumbled up the snowbank and struggled to run, but the two feet of snow was coated in half an inch of ice. She managed to take three steps on the slippery surface before her foot plunged into snow up to her knee. She yanked her leg back and lost her boot in the snow. *No!* She dropped to her hands and knees, and dug for her boot. Her fingers brushed the cuff. She tugged it out and put it back on.

But she was too late. Her attacker tackled her from behind.

He pressed a knee into her back and spoke in her ear, his voice deep and as rough as sandpaper. "Tell me where Charlotte Finn is and I'll let you go."

Charlotte Finn? Her head swam. Charlotte was the history student Piper had briefly shared an apartment with in college six years ago. She hadn't seen the snobby, slender blonde since Charlotte had asked if she could come visit The Downs for Christmas that year— and then robbed them.

"I don't know." She shook her head. "Honestly, I don't."

"You're lying." He flipped her over and pushed her back into the snow.

She tried to yell, but her voice broke. "I have no idea where Charlotte is!"

Piper kicked him hard with both legs. He grunted and fell off her. She struggled to her feet and kept running. The string around her neck had loosened just enough for her to see a couple of inches under the bag and to gulp in a deep, pain-filled breath. She felt her shins smack against something—the barn steps. She found the railing and then ran her gloved hands along it. The old rotting wood was a mess of splinters and nails. If she could just loop the string around her wrists on something sharp, she might be able to snap herself free.

"I know she's here." Footsteps landed hard behind her. "You're going to tell me where she is."

He grabbed her jacket and yanked her around. For a split second she could see his wrist—the blurry lines of a bear tattoo and the word *Kodiak*. He grabbed ahold of the string around her neck and yanked her back hard, cutting off her windpipe. Pain shot through her lungs. Her hands tore free of their bonds and she clutched at her throat.

She couldn't breathe.

"I'm not playing around." He choked her harder. "Charlotte's here. Somewhere. You think you're helping her out by hiding her and lying to me? I got too much on the line to let this go and if I've got to murder all her friends to make her show herself, I will. So, you're to tell me where she is. Right now. Or I will kill you."

There was the metallic clink of a butterfly knife. Then she felt the tip of the blade pushing through the bag and into the back of her neck.

Oh God, help me. Please.

A horn split the air. The loud, insistent blare sounded as if someone was leaning on it with their full weight. Her attacker swore and shoved her off the steps. She fell into the snow and gasped as air filled her lungs again. The honking grew louder. Then she heard a man shouting, but she couldn't make out the words.

There was the long, painful screech of brakes.

Then a deafening, splintering crunch.

TWO

The side of the old wooden barn rushed up toward the windshield. Benjamin yanked the steering wheel hard to the left and prayed for just enough traction to avoid ramming straight through it. He spun and barely cleared the corner. But the brick chimney wasn't so fortunate. The truck crashed through the chimney sideways. Bricks rained down onto the hood, cracks spreading across the windshield like sudden frost.

The seat belt snapped him back against the seat.

He gasped in a breath. Well, that was either the bravest or the most foolish thing he'd ever done. His attempt at a steady but fast descent down the hill had turned into more of a slide than he'd wanted. But it was more than worth the risk if it meant saving Piper's life.

Where is she now? Is she all right?

At least he'd thought to let the dog out before attempting the hill.

Benjamin yanked open the driver's door and leaped out into the snow, throwing the door closed behind him. The windshield exploded, showering the inside of the truck with glass.

He cupped his gloved hands around his mouth. "Piper! Shout if you can hear me!"

He yanked his hat down farther, wrapped his scarf twice around his face and pushed his way through the snow.

A huge man dashed around the corner and froze. A battered black winter coat hid his form and a black ski mask covered his face. But Benjamin could clearly see the knife clenched in his outstretched hand. Benjamin leaped for it, forcing the masked man's arm into the air as he wrenched the weapon from his grasp. The masked man punched out hard, catching him in the jaw.

Benjamin stumbled back. But he managed to keep hold of the attacker's knife.

The man gave up and bolted for the tree line. The urge to chase after him surged through Benjamin. But finding Piper was all that mattered now.

"Hey, Piper!" He ran around the side of the barn. "Piper! Where are you?"

No answer but the howl of the wind and the ice pellets smacking the ground.

Then he saw her. Facedown in a heavy snowbank beside the barn stairs. He ran for her, slid one strong arm under her and pulled her to her feet. When he saw the bag tied over her head, his throat tightened so he couldn't even speak. He unwrapped the string from around her neck as quickly as he dared and pulled the sack off her head.

His gaze fell on Piper's face. Chestnut hair fell loose around her shoulders. Her huge, dark eyes looked up into his. She gasped in a deep breath.

Then she punched him squarely in the gut. And ran.

Benjamin felt the air rush from his lungs. "Piper...

Wait…" His winded chest struggled for breath. "It's okay! It's me—"

"Benjamin?" She turned back. Sleet poured down her slender frame. Her eyes scrunched as if trying to focus.

He realized she wasn't wearing her glasses and could barely see without them.

"Yeah, Piper," he said softly, yanking off his hat and scarf. "It's okay. It's me. Benjamin."

"Thank God!" A smile crossed her lips as her eyes rose upward in prayer. Then her gaze turned back to his. "I'm so glad you're here."

He crossed the snow toward her, feeling that odd lump in his throat grow even bigger.

Piper had been the first person to really call him "Benjamin." She'd known exactly who he was the moment they met. Most Ontarians between the ages of thirteen and twenty-eight seemed to, thanks to a particularly horrendous documentary about his accident that was regularly shown in high school assemblies. But in that moment, when she'd been play-fighting with the dog in the entrance to his store and he'd rushed over to greet her, she'd stretched out her hand and said, "Do you prefer Benji or Benjamin?" As if the fact that his sister, his friends and every single news outlet still referred to him by his childhood nickname hadn't settled the matter. It was the most rebelliously thoughtful question he'd ever been asked.

"It's okay. You're safe now." He pulled off his gloves and let his bare fingers brush her hair. "Are you okay?"

"Yeah, I'm okay." She grabbed his left hand and held it tightly. Somehow her voice managed to sound a bit stronger than his. "What happened to the guy who attacked me?"

"Gone." His eyes glanced toward the empty tree line. "He ran."

"What did he look like?"

"Tall. Heavyset. Black ski mask. Tattoo on his wrist but I couldn't make it out."

"It was a bear," she said, "and the word *Kodiak*. But I have no idea who he was. He said he was looking for someone I used to know, a woman named Charlotte. But I haven't seen her in years."

She didn't move. Neither did he. They both just stood there, knee-deep in ice and snow, with sleet smacking against their bodies and their hands holding on to each other. Her face was turned up toward his, her cheeks flushed. *She's beyond beautiful.* The thought hit him from out of the blue. There was a quality to her that defied his ability to find adjectives to describe her. He wanted to pull her close, wrap both arms around her and shield her body from the storm.

But he'd never hugged Piper before. Sure, they'd hung out as pals. Great pals. Which was different than a hugging kind of friendship.

Her free hand brushed his beard, as if to double-check he was really there. "But how about you? Are you okay? Where's the dog? I thought I heard something crash into the barn."

"Don't worry. Everything's fine." He pulled her hand away from his face, stepped back and held both her hands together in front of him at arm's length, with what he hoped felt like a reassuring squeeze. "I let the dog out at the top of the hill so he's probably racing through the trees right now. My truck is mostly okay. I didn't spin out of control so much as do a fast and calculated skid." Because, in that second, it was a choice between watching her die from a distance or getting down the hill fast enough to save her. "Now, we need to call the police. My cell phone can't get a signal."

"Mine might. I dropped it in the barn. Plus, that's where I lost my glasses. My vision's pretty blurry without them."

He stretched out his arm to guide her up the stairs. Instead, she let go and started walking. He followed her into the barn. The smell of old wood and hay filled his senses. Lights flickered to life above them, revealing rows of stacked chairs, folding tables and boxes of Christmas decorations. A loft lay on one side, with bales of hay tucked underneath. He spotted a fireplace against the far wall, but it was entirely cemented up on the inside and probably hadn't been used in decades. At least he hadn't driven into the chimney of a working fireplace. Something crunched under his foot. He bent down and picked up the remains of a blue-and-silver decoration.

"Watch your step. He jumped me the moment I stepped in the door." She started feeling around on the floor. He unzipped his ski jacket and knelt down beside her. The wind howled, shaking the door in its door frame. "I hit my head and lost consciousness. I never even saw it coming."

All the more reason to be thankful he was leaving Harry behind as a guard dog. "Isn't it a bit late to be down here all by yourself?"

"I've been walking down the hill to the barn, alone, ever since I was a kid." She rolled her eyes. "Even before Uncle Des put the path and lights in. Which I think he only did because Aunt Cass was worried I'd break my neck running through the trees in the dark."

"You used to live with them, right?"

"Yeah. The Downs is theirs and I run it for them. They've had to temporarily move in to a retirement building in town because of health problems." She sighed and sat back on her heels. "Found my phone. Parts of it, anyway."

He looked down at the pieces in her hand. It looked as if someone had stomped on it. Glancing behind her, he spotted her glasses. He carefully bent them back into shape and cleaned them on the corner of his shirt before handing them to her. "Here you go. Now, what kind of security do you have if he comes back?"

"Just the usual locks on the doors and windows." She slid her glasses on. Then she grabbed a box of Christmas things from the floor and carried it across the barn, scooping stray decorations off the floor as she went. "I have three guests at The Downs right now, so I won't be alone. But there's absolutely no reason for anyone to come back here looking for Charlotte. If she was in trouble I'm the last person she'd go to for help. We weren't even friends."

She set the box down beside a pile of other ones. "Charlotte was just my arrogant, former roommate. Six years ago, she talked me into letting her come stay at The Downs by telling me she could prove it had some hidden, rum-running past and had been used as a speakeasy during Prohibition. But she was probably just using me to get a break from her abusive, controlling ex-boyfriend. He was some nasty piece of work."

"Nasty enough to threaten to kill you in order to find her six years later?" he asked.

"I don't know." Piper shrugged. "I never met him. She called him Alpha—like the head of an animal pack.

He called her constantly, expected her to drop everything and run to him, and sometimes sent really creepy
presents like dead flowers. But he was also really financially generous when he wanted to be. Rich and twisted.
Even if this Kodiak guy isn't Alpha, he could be a sign
her taste in men hasn't changed." She crossed the barn
toward him. "But either way, any sympathy I had for her
disappeared the moment she repaid our kindness by robbing The Downs, smashing years' worth of handmade
Christmas decorations into tiny pieces and knocking
our tree through the front window—"

The door slammed shut so hard the whole barn
shook.

The lights went out.

Her heart was beating so hard she was almost afraid
Benjamin could hear it. He'd thrown his arms around
her and now the warmth of his chest was pressed up
against hers, the strength of his arms wrapped around
her shoulders. Right then she needed it. She could barely
keep her knees from buckling.

"Hey, it's okay." She forced herself to step back out
of his arms. "It's probably just the wind coupled with
some ice on the power lines."

"Maybe it's nothing. But maybe it's something." Benjamin's hand slid down her arm and squeezed hers. "Either way, get behind me and stay close."

Tempting. But no. She'd spent way too long trying
to rid herself of the dizzying butterflies that soared
through her veins whenever Benjamin was near. She
wasn't about to lose her head now. Sure, back on the
island last summer she'd thought their relationship was
heading somewhere romantic. Right up until he'd taken

her out to dinner her last night on the island only to blindside her with the news that he was determined to remain a commitment-free bachelor for the rest of his life.

"Power goes out around here all the time in the winter." She pulled her fingers out of his grip. "It usually comes right back within minutes. But even if it is someone dangerous, I'm going to meet it head-on."

Benjamin didn't step back. "Look, Piper. I know you're plenty strong—"

"Yes, I am. Just because one thug managed to get the jump on me doesn't suddenly mean I'm helpless." She sounded more defensive than she meant to. But the fact that Benjamin was probably pretty used to taking charge in bad situations didn't mean she was some damsel in distress, counting on a handsome man to save her. Especially not the kind of a man who was in a hurry to leave. "Don't forget, I was a pretty fierce hockey player and not half-bad at mixed martial arts, too. Both times I took out guys every bit as big as Kodiak."

The only reason she didn't compete nationally was the cost of the training and the time she'd be away from The Downs, where she was needed to help run the place.

"I remember." His voice dropped. "But I nearly lost my sister, Meg, to the Raincoat Killer last year. I'd never forgive myself if anything happened to you. Not when there was a chance that I could've stepped up and done something to protect you."

The lights flickered on again. There was the furious yip of barking and the scramble of paws. Piper flung the barn door open, then dropped to one knee as Harry bolted through. She buried her face in the husky's soft fur. "Hey there, guard dog. Welcome to The Downs."

Benjamin looked out. "Well, if there was anyone there, Harry frightened them off."

"Thanks for bringing him down. I think he's exactly what I need around this place." She gripped the dog's collar and stood. Time for her to call the police and for Benjamin to get back on the road.

"I'm going to miss him like crazy." Benjamin followed her out of the barn. "But sadly, once I'm on my boat, I've got no room for Harry."

Or a relationship. Or a family. Or emotional complications of any kind.

He'd told her so that last night on the island. It didn't matter what kind of fireworks that man set off inside her chest, Benjamin couldn't even commit to a dog.

They rounded the corner and Piper gasped—his truck was a mess of scrunched metal and broken glass. "I thought you said everything was okay."

The chimney had a huge chunk missing from one side. Bricks dented the hood of his large black pickup. Yes, she'd heard the sound of a collision. But he'd been so reassuring she'd just trusted him when he told her everything was okay.

"The truck will be fine," he said. "A new side panel and a fresh windshield and it'll be good to go. I'm really sorry about the chimney. Hopefully it's nothing a good masonry job won't fix. I'd offer to do it myself if it wasn't knee-deep in snow and I didn't have places to be. I just hope it won't be a problem for your Christmas Eve shindig."

"It's more than a shindig." She took a deep breath and reminded herself that none of this was Benjamin's fault, and that he was even more inconvenienced than she was. "It's called Christmas Eve at The Downs. The purpose is to provide a really awesome potluck dinner and carol singing for people in the community who have nowhere else to go. Aunt Cass started it twenty-five years ago. This is the first year I'm managing it on my own. The barn's really old and I really should have gotten a new roof put on it this year. But the priority has been saving up to renovate the bed-and-breakfast."

The sooner she could get Uncle Des and Aunt Cass out of that awful seniors' residence the better.

"*Torchlight News* did a big article on your renovation plans, right?" Benjamin asked. "Because your house was declared a heritage site of historical value, you needed to apply to get special permission?" He brushed the glass off the driver's seat and climbed in.

"Yup. The Downs is over a hundred years old. We're pretty isolated, so there are rumors that during American Prohibition, people used to sneak across the lake and fill their boats up with bottles of illegal rum out of this very barn. Some even say there was a full-fledged speakeasy lounge with drinks and music running in The Downs. All these people would supposedly boat across the lake and sneak up through our woods in their finest evening wear. But no one's ever found any evidence. Not even so much as an empty rum bottle or lost earring in the trees. Trust me, I looked."

As a little girl she'd combed The Downs for some hidden stash of jewelry or money. As an adult, she'd be happy to just see The Downs increase in value enough they could get a loan to cover renovations.

Benjamin pulled the truck back. The corner of the hood was crumpled and the whole right side was dented. But still the engine ran smoothly and the air bag hadn't deployed.

THREE

To his surprise, Piper blinked. Her hand rose to her lips as if his question had somehow caught her off guard. "Oh. Sure. Of course. I've only got three guests staying right now. I can definitely house one more."

Okay, and what was he missing now? It had seemed like a pretty straightforward thing to ask. After all, she ran a bed-and-breakfast, and it was unlikely a mechanic would get him back on the road before morning. He turned off the truck and climbed out. "Well, as long as it's no problem and won't cause you any extra trouble."

"No, no trouble at all." She wasn't meeting his eye. "It's the least I can do, considering you probably saved my life."

Alrighty, then. Benjamin yanked a tarp out of the backseat and began tying it down over the missing windshield to keep the worst of the snow out. Truth be told, he'd feel a whole lot better staying close by in case Kodiak was still lurking around. Something told him that memory of Piper down in the snow with a bag over her head would haunt his nightmares for a long time. There was a tug on the tarp. He looked up. Piper had grabbed the other side and was tying it down on the passenger side.

Her eyes cut to the National Hockey League team logo on his bag. A smile curved on her lips. "You're just lucky you saved my life before I remembered you supported our hockey rivals in Montreal."

He chuckled. Yeah, he hadn't forgotten just how passionate she was about cheering on Toronto. "Well, as long as you don't high stick me, I promise to leave all conversations about Stanley Cup history at the door."

She rolled her eyes. They started up the steep, narrow path through the trees. Harry ran beside them for a while then disappeared on ahead. Benjamin tried to hitch his duffel bag higher on his shoulder and just barely managed to keep from knocking into her.

"That's a pretty big bag for visiting a few friends," she said. "I thought you believed in traveling light."

"I do." He swung it around to the other shoulder. "Actually, this is everything I'm taking with me to Australia. Passport, airline ticket, travel money—if it's crossing the world with me, it's in here."

The sun had set behind the snow. Motion sensor lights wound through the trees ahead of them, flickering on as they neared. He reached the top of the hill and looked out. Snow-covered trees flowed down the slope behind them, spreading all the way out over the lake. It was breathtaking.

"On a clearer day, you can see the American shoreline," Piper said. "Uncle Des and Aunt Cass married in the south of England. He had what he thought was a temporary job at a company in Niagara and they moved out here. Aunt Cass named The Downs after the South Downs, this range of hills near the village she's from. They got the property in a foreclosure sale actually.

Took them years to sort through all the junk the previous owners left behind."

"But sadly no illegal rum in the cellar or stacks of secret cash in the wardrobe?"

She shook her head. "Nope."

He turned toward the house. The Downs was three stories tall, with lead piping on the windows, peaked roofs and shuttered doors opening onto small balconies. Christmas lights wrapped around the windows and balconies, and looped around the fire escape that ran all the way from the ground floor to a round window high in the roof peak. "So this would be your fairy-tale castle?"

She stopped walking. "What did you just say?"

"I seem to remember you telling me that you were born in England, too, but that you and your mom moved here to live when you were really little. So, you used to pretend you were secretly an English princess and The Downs was your castle."

She paused for a moment then shook her head. "I can't believe I told you that."

If anything, she sounded disappointed with herself. But why? They'd talked for hours during those four days last summer. She'd told him all sorts of things about herself. He in turn had confessed stuff about himself that nobody else knew. Like how he'd decided he was never going to have a wife or family.

"I was one when I moved in here actually," she said. "We were pretty broke. My father left us a couple of weeks before Christmas and my mom had no way to pay the rent without him. The British expression is 'he did a runner,' so for the longest time I thought he'd literally leaped out a window and ran. Our flight landed

Christmas Eve. We were the first two wanderers to be welcomed at Christmas Eve at The Downs."

He followed Piper past a towering woodpile, through a small back door and into the garage. His eyes ran over racks of ice-hockey equipment. A kayak, canoe and two surfboards lay on beams above their heads, and there was camping equipment on wall shelves. Steel-toed hiking boots hung on a peg by the door, next to two pairs of boxing gloves, some climbing gear and what looked like a heavy wool cloak. All of the gear looked high quality, well loved and as if it hadn't been touched in ages.

"So, if you keep the bed-and-breakfast open over Christmas, when do you take your own holidays?"

"I don't really." She pulled off her coat, then pushed her foggy glasses up onto the top of her head. "The Downs is open and running 365 days a year."

Okay, he heard what she was saying, but there was something wrong with this picture. They were standing in a garage surrounded by incredible sports equipment. Sure, living in the Niagara region meant she could probably get in a bit of skating or cross-country skiing. But there were only so many times a person could hit the same patch of earth before wanting to try something new. And she could hardly surf or camp without taking a day off.

"Yes, but the whole reason we met is because you were on holiday on Manitoulin Island this past summer—"

"No, I was on the island for four days while my uncle was here helping movers pack up their things so they could move into the seniors' home. My aunt's health is poor, and a friend of hers who lived on the island invited her to stay for a few days. She wasn't able to make the trip alone so I went with her." She shrugged. "I'm going to need to run this place nonstop at capacity if I have any hope of starting the renovations by this summer. Even once they're done, my uncle and aunt are going to need me around on a daily basis. Like I said, they have health problems."

"Okay, but what kind of health problems?"

"My uncle has arthritis in his hands and arms. Not too bad, but he's also seventy-two. My aunt's a lot younger but she has mobility problems. She needs help doing things and getting places." She wiped her glasses on her shirt and then slid them back on. But she still wasn't looking at him. "If it's okay with you, I'd rather not go into it right now."

He ran his hand through his hair. Why did it feel as if this conversation was one wrong sentence away from turning into an argument? His sister's anxiety disorder had kept him from pursuing his own dreams for way too long, so he should be the last person to judge anyone else's commitment to family. It was definitely time for a subject change. He looked around the garage and spotted a small tractor by the wall with a snowplow on the front. "Nice piece of machinery. I'm guessing you clear your own snow?"

"Always. I also rake my own leaves in the fall and mow my own lawn in the summer."

"Well, how about I plow the driveway and hill, while you call the police?"

She opened the kitchen door, pulled a key chain off the wall and tossed it to him. "Thanks. I'm also going to call my uncle and aunt, and the mechanic about your truck."

"Great. Tell him I have insurance but I'm happy to

pay out of pocket if that speeds things up. Anything I can do to get out of here faster."

"Will do." She walked into the kitchen.

Benjamin opened the garage door and stared out at the dark, snowy night. What was it with Piper? There was this weird tension between them that he couldn't get his head around.

He'd told himself that when the time came to leave Canada, he'd do his best to make peace with everyone he left behind. But how could he make peace with Piper if he didn't even know what he'd done wrong?

The steady clacking sound of fingers on a typewriter echoed through The Downs, like some kind of robust combination of music and water torture. Tobias Kasper wrote books on tactical warfare and was the kind of guest who treated the entirety of The Downs as an extension of his suite. Right now, the short, rotund middle-aged man sat in the middle of the living room, sporting a paisley bow tie and the kind of vest that some people called a waistcoat. He was pounding the keys of a machine that had to be at least sixty years old.

Piper nodded to him politely and closed the kitchen door. The Downs's galley kitchen was much smaller than she would've liked, while the living room was huge, with an old brick fireplace and a huge wooden staircase leading to a sweeping second-floor balcony. When it came time to renovate, they'd be knocking down the wall between the two rooms. But right now, she was thankful for something to muffle the noise.

Her nerves were frayed enough as it was. She'd thought her heart was going to leap into her throat when Benjamin asked if he could take a suite for the night, and it finally hit her that he'd be staying around a little while longer. Benjamin had absolutely no idea the effect he had on her. And he was never going to know.

The phone began to ring. Piper was about to let it ring through to the answering machine, when her gaze caught the name on the display: Silver Halls Retirement Home. She grabbed the phone. "Hello?"

"Piper, honey?" It was Aunt Cass.

Piper smiled. "Hi, Aunt Cass. I see you finally managed to get a turn on the landline phone."

Laughter trickled down the line. "I was about to use my cell phone. But your uncle started going on about saving minutes and I didn't know if you'd gotten my text."

Piper's sparkling, vibrant, sixty-three year old aunt was nine years younger than Piper's uncle, and so very young at heart. Aunt Cass hadn't wanted to do anything even close to retire when persistent, unexplained numbness in her legs and then her arms forced her and Uncle Des to move out of The Downs into the only available rental place in town where everything was accessible on the ground floor.

"I've got an appointment for more tests at the hospital in Niagara Falls on January 12," her aunt informed her.

Piper grabbed a pen and wrote it on the calendar. "No problem. I'll be able to drive you."

What kind of health problems? Benjamin had asked the question so casually, as if the answer was as simple as a sprained ankle or chicken pox. It had taken everything inside her not to groan, "We don't know! That's the problem!" She wasn't even sure when her aunt's limbs first stopped cooperating with her brain, like a frustrated marionette with intermittent strings. But after sudden numbness in her legs sent Aunt Cass tumbling down the stairs into the living room last summer, a broken arm and nasty bruises had woken them all up to the reality that their lives were going to change. Since then it had been a string of doctors, tests and possible diagnoses like amyotrophic lateral sclerosis, multiple sclerosis, Parkinson's disease. And prayers. Lots of prayers.

Piper ran her hand along her neck. It was tender. Now she was about to tell them something that would make life even more complicated than it already was. "Now, Aunt Cass, please don't worry, but I was just… accosted by a trespasser down by the barn."

"Desmond! Get your coat!"

"No, wait! It's okay." Piper waved her aunt down, even though she couldn't see her through the phone. "He's gone and I'm fine! I am going to call the police and file a report, but he was just looking for Charlotte Finn."

"The sad, blonde girl who liked puzzle books?"

Trust her aunt to remember Charlotte as the girl who was sad and liked puzzles, as opposed to the one who'd smashed every single one of Aunt Cass's cherished handmade nativity figures on the fireplace mantel. "Yes, her. I haven't seen her or heard from her in years, and I told him so."

"Was it her young man?" Suddenly Uncle Des was on the line and Piper realized her aunt must be holding the phone up between them.

"I don't know," Piper said. "I never met him."

"Tall. Big shoulders. Young lad."

"You met Alpha?" Piper blinked. "Six years since she robbed us and you never told me that!"

"Didn't know who the guy was. Just saw her smooching someone in the woods out my window one night when I was locking up. Told her to knock it off and come inside. He ran off and I never saw his face. I didn't think it was anybody's business. But I gave the police a description then and I'm happy to do so again now."

"You come by tomorrow and fill us in," Aunt Cass said. "In the meantime, you might want to see if Dominic Bravo wants to rent a suite. You remember him? From youth group?"

"Yeah, of course I do." Dominic was a great guy. Sure, the former high school athlete was pretty quiet and shy, and floundered in school. But when Charlotte's robbery rampage had included knocking Piper unconscious, Dominic had been the one who'd realized Piper was in trouble and had come to find her. "Didn't even realize he was back in town."

"He's back in town for a few weeks studying for the police academy. His grandmother says he's staying with his sister and all her little ones right now, sleeping on their pullout couch."

"Good for him! My friend Benjamin is taking the final suite for tonight, but I'll keep Dominic in mind. Speaking of which, I really must call the police now. I'll come by and see you tomorrow."

She said her goodbyes and hung up the phone. When she heard a floorboard creak behind her, she turned. Tobias was standing in the doorway, leaning on his cane. As far as she could tell the cane was simply part of his eccentric style and fashion sense, as opposed to something he actually needed to walk.

"I'm sorry," he said, "I couldn't help but overhear. You have a problem with intruders?"

Piper stepped back. She hadn't even thought through

how she was going to tell Tobias and her other two guests about what had happened with Kodiak. "Yes, I was just about to call the police. Then I thought I'd call you, Gavin and Trisha together in the living room to update you all."

He ran one hand through his salt-and-pepper hair. "You know, rumor has it that back in World War II, the enemy used the most inventive booby traps against the Allies, including exploding soap, oil paintings and chocolate. It's all about thinking like a predator, Piper."

"How interesting." She smiled politely. "But I'm sure if we do beef up security we'll find something a little less dramatic." A building as old as The Downs tended to attract a lot of quirky folk, but exploding chocolate was definitely a new one. "Speaking of history, have you ever heard the rumor that The Downs used to be used in alcohol smuggling?"

"Oh, my expertise is in warfare, not local history." Tobias shook his head. "But, I'd have thought most of the action took place closer to either Michigan or New York. This stretch of Lake Erie was supposed to be fairly uninteresting."

Downright boring is the way she'd have been tempted to describe it, if it wasn't for Charlotte bringing unwanted chaos to her door.

The next couple of hours passed in a blur. Cops came to take their statements. A tow truck took Benjamin's vehicle to the garage. She called her other two guests, married lawyers Gavin and Trisha, but only got their voice mail. Tobias typed though it all.

And Benjamin…

She leaned back on the couch and looked down at her tea. Benjamin had been everywhere at once, plowing the drive, sanding the steps as the freezing rain continued to fall, taking coats as people came in and giving them back as they left again. He'd even found his own linens and made his own bed when she pointed him in the direction of his suite.

Before she knew it, the clock struck eleven.

"Why don't you have a Christmas tree?" Benjamin's voice cut through her thoughts.

She looked up and only then realized that they were now alone in the living room. "I put so much work into decorating the barn, I didn't really plan to do anything for inside the house. I'm going to cut down a tree for the barn tomorrow."

The fire dimmed in the hearth. Benjamin added some kindling, then got down on his stomach and blew on the flame. The dog promptly laid his head on top of him. *Don't let yourself get too comfortable, pup. He's not staying long.*

"How did everything go when you called your sister?" she asked.

"Okay." He sat up and the dog moved with him. "But she sounded really stressed. I should be there making things easier for her, not adding to her problems. It's bad enough I'm the guy who triggered her anxiety disorder to begin with by some stupid snowmobile accident. I don't want to be the guy who makes her relapse right before her wedding."

There was a bitter edge to his voice that she wasn't used to hearing, almost as if he was simultaneously talking and smacking himself on the back of the head.

"I get that." She leaned forward. "But don't beat yourself up. You saved my life from a violent creep today. And that snowmobile accident happened way back when you were a kid."

"I was fifteen." He turned back to the fire. "I was old enough to know better."

Piper pressed her lips together. Benjamin had been driving underage, on a highway, without a license and without a helmet. Those were a lot of mistakes to go through life hanging over his head. The older friend he'd been snowmobiling with hadn't even survived the crash and the media coverage had been harsh and relentless. Long before she'd met Benjamin, she'd known exactly who he was—her generation's poster child for foolishness.

"Well, I'm going to sleep." Benjamin stood. "I've got a long drive tomorrow."

"Good night." She started up the stairs shortly after she'd taken care of the fire. The Downs had three unique guest suites on the second floor, but her room was up another flight of stairs in a large loft space with slanted ceilings and round windows.

When she opened the door that led to a flight of stairs to her loft, she felt fur brush past her ankles, then Harry bounded onto her bed under the eaves. She snapped her fingers and pointed to the stairs. "Sorry, dog. I need to sleep. I can't afford to be woken up in the middle of the night just because you feel like wandering."

The husky gave her a pointed look with sky-blue eyes that looked like his owner's. What had she been thinking inviting a constant reminder of Benjamin to move into her home?

"Tell you what. I'll get a doggie door installed soon. Okay?" She let him down and locked the door behind him. Then she changed into a fresh T-shirt and track pants, set her glasses down on the bedside table and slid under the blankets.

"Thank You, God, for bringing Benjamin here to save me," she prayed as a sigh slipped through her lips. "Now help me protect my heart until he leaves."

Exhausted sleep swept over her before she'd barely finished her prayer.

A creak jolted her awake.

Piper opened her eyes and sat up.

Her alarm clock read four in the morning. The room was cold.

But it wasn't the temperature that sent chills down her spine. It was the figure was standing at the foot of her bed.

FOUR

Fear gripped Piper's body, pushing her back against the headboard. The intruder was nothing but an indistinct shape in the darkness. But she could see it. Standing there. Inches away from the bed. Not moving. Just breathing.

She reached toward her glasses.

"Don't move." A whisper hissed in the darkness.

Piper's hand froze on the nightstand.

"Don't scream, either. You just stay quiet, okay?" It wasn't the same voice as the man in the diamond ski mask. No, this one sounded uncertain. Agitated. Even nervous. Definitely higher-pitched, too. Female. "I don't want to hurt you. But I've got a gun, okay? I'll shoot you if I have to."

"Got it." Piper slid her body even farther back until she could feel her headboard press into her shoulder blades. She didn't know whether to believe the intruder, but didn't want to risk it, either. There were heavy wooden doors on the bedrooms below and thick carpets to muffle sound. If she screamed would anyone even hear her?

Help me, Lord. I'm terrified.

The intruder was jumpy, too, and even seemed to be pacing. Knowing she was frightened, panicking and apparently armed didn't make Piper feel any safer. How had anyone even broken in to her room? Piper's eyes adjusted to the darkness, just enough to make out shapes on her bedside table. A cold breeze swept up her arms. Wind howled in the darkness. The intruder must have climbed the fire escape and come through her window. Piper's fingers crept across the nightstand. "This house is full of people. Just leave. Now. Nobody needs to get hurt."

"I said don't move." The shadow moved closer. Her voice shook. "I have a gun, okay? I'm just here looking for something. I'm going to get it and leave."

Something or *someone*? Piper took a deep breath and fought the nerves from her voice. "What are you looking for?"

No answer.

"Who told you you'd find it here? Did he have a bear tattoo?"

Again, no answer. Just the wheezy, shallow gasps of someone battling for breath.

Piper gritted her teeth and beat down her fear even as it threatened to swallow the words from her lungs.

"Charlotte, is that you?"

The only response was a hysterical giggle, halfway between a laugh and a sob.

Piper's hand slid along the nightstand.

I'm sitting; she's standing. She's got a weapon. I don't.

Lord, I need a split-second distraction.

"I said, don't move!" The voice rose.

"And I said *leave*. Now. Whatever it is you think you're after here nobody needs to get hurt."

The shadow moved closer. She was slender. Long hair curled at her shoulders. The outline of a gun waved in front of Piper's eyes.

"I said I don't want to hurt you. I don't want to hurt anyone. But I will if I have to!" A face swam into view, featureless except for the eyes and mouth visible through the crude holes of a blue ski mask. The gun brushed Piper's forehead. "He'll make me kill you."

Whoever "he" was, he'd apparently sent a terrified coward to break into Piper's room and threaten her with a weapon she probably didn't even know how to use. Piper prayed her next question would hit its mark. "Who? Alpha? Did Alpha send you?"

The intruder leaned back with a gasp, as quickly and violently as if Piper had just slapped her. In one fluid motion Piper snatched the lamp off her bedside table and smashed it into the masked woman's head. The intruder screamed. Piper rolled off the bed and landed on her hands and knees. That's when she heard the barking below her. Harry was downstairs trying to get through her door.

A gloved hand grabbed a fistful of Piper's hair and yanked hard. Pain shot through Piper's skull. The woman bent down and hissed in Piper's ear. "Don't you dare say that name again. You don't understand who Alpha is. You don't have any clue what kind of man you're dealing with here!"

Maybe not.

But apparently Alpha didn't understand what kind of woman he was dealing with in Piper, either.

Piper's fingers grasped the hockey-goalie stick under

her bed. She leaped up and with both hands she cross-checked her attacker hard in the chest. Her attacker stumbled and fell. Piper snatched up her glasses, pushed them onto her nose and then smacked the switch for the overhead light. Light filled the loft. The intruder was female, slightly shorter than Piper and thinner. Long blond curls poured out from under a navy blue ski mask. A small handgun shook in her gloved hands.

Blonde Bambi with bullets.

Just as she suspected, the bedroom window was open, and freezing rain poured through. From downstairs the barking grew louder.

Blondie was standing between her and the stairs. "Look, it's not too late for everybody to get out of this okay. Just go downstairs and make that dog shut up. Then tell everyone that everything's okay."

"Why would I do that?" Piper took a step back, holding the hockey stick firm in her grasp. There were four other people in the bed-and-breakfast below her right now and Benjamin was the only one she was sure could take care of himself.

"Because like I said, I don't want to hurt anyone! I just need to look around." She clutched the gun with both hands. "Just…just go shut the dog up. Then come back, lie still and stay quiet. I'll search your stuff and go."

I don't believe you.

Piper could hear the dog's paws scrambling as if Harry was now trying to dig his way through the door. Then she heard knocking at her door, and the knob rattled. Benjamin called her name.

"Benjamin! Call 911!" She shouted so loudly her throat ached. "There's an armed intruder in the bed-

and-breakfast. Tell everyone to stay in their rooms and lock their doors!"

Green eyes narrowed inside the ski mask. "You should've have done that."

Maybe not, but I have more confidence in my ability to wield this hockey stick than I do in your ability to aim that gun.

Piper tightened her grasp. "Drop the gun, climb back out that window and run while you can."

"It's too late for that." The blonde's voice rose. "You don't understand him."

"You mean Alpha?"

The blonde closed her eyes and raised the gun.

Piper swung the hockey stick as a gunshot split the air.

Benjamin threw his shoulder into Piper's bedroom door, just as a bullet splintered the wood above his head. He leaped back against the wall, yanking Harry by the collar.

"Everyone, back!" He glanced behind him. Tobias was leaning out his suite door in a lush velvet bathrobe, like a posh rubbernecker on a highway accident. "Please."

When Harry had leaped onto his bed and started barking, Benjamin had presumed a raccoon had gotten into the garbage. But the dog hadn't been willing to shush. When Harry gripped his arm gently but firmly with his teeth Benjamin had realized something was terribly wrong.

Help me get to Piper, God. Help me save her.

Piper screamed. The sound seemed to shatter his heart in his rib cage.

"What in the blazes is going on here?" An irritated voice behind him spoke. "My wife is pregnant. We're trying to sleep!"

Benjamin wheeled around, coming face-to-face with a tall, angry young man with jet-black hair. He figured it was Gavin, staying here with his wife, Trisha. "Go call the police. Now! Lock your door and don't come out!"

Then he turned back to Piper's door without waiting for an answer. As much as he hated the idea of running into gunfire, he could hardly leave Piper alone up there. He lowered his head and charged the door. As his body hit the center of the wood the door cracked and flew open. Piper was crouched halfway up the stairs. Her hands were raised above her head, clutching two ends of a broken hockey stick.

"Benjamin?" She spoke his name without even turning.

"Yeah." He stretched one hand out into the empty space between them. "I'm here."

Harry pressed against Benjamin's leg, a deep growl rumbling in his throat. Benjamin grabbed the dog's collar and held it firm. His gaze rose to the masked, armed blonde at the top of the stairs. "Drop the gun and let her go. Nobody needs to get hurt."

"I can't!" She pointed the barrel of her gun directly at Piper's chest. The weapon shook, as if it had come to life and her hands were fighting to control it. "I don't want to shoot her but I will if you make me."

He heard a bedroom door open behind him. The blonde fired. Piper tumbled backward down the stairs. Benjamin let Harry go and caught her with both arms.

"My cell phone isn't working." Gavin's head peeked out a doorway.

Close your mouth and close the door! Benjamin fought the urge to yell. But the top of the stairs was empty now. The gun-wielding blonde was now nowhere to be seen. Neither was Harry.

"Fortunately, Trisha got the landline to work." Gavin was clutching a glass bottle of amber liquid. It sloshed. *Please, no! Don't let Gavin be getting drunk right now!* "The police said the roads are closed due to the ice storm, so it might take them a while to get here."

Piper slid out of Benjamin's arms. "Gavin, you and Trisha stay in your room, lock the door and don't come out until the police arrive."

Something inside Benjamin was fighting the urge to tell Piper to go hide, too, and let him handle this, even though he suspected she wasn't about to listen. Silence fell from above. He slapped his leg and whistled, but the dog didn't come back.

"Is that Charlotte?" he asked.

"I honestly don't know. She didn't give any reaction when I mentioned the guy with the bear tattoo. But I'm pretty sure she knows who Alpha is." Piper snatched up the pieces of broken hockey stick from the bottom of the stairs. "The Charlotte I knew wasn't quite that thin and her blond hair was straight, not curly. But those are all cosmetic changes and I don't know for sure without seeing her face. Whoever she is, she clearly doesn't know how to aim a weapon. She's terrified and out of control." Determination and fire flashed in the dark depths of Piper's eyes. "We need to find a way to hold her until the cops get here."

He reached out to hold her back but Piper had already pulled away and looked ready to charge back up the loft.

"My bedroom window was open and I'm guessing

she'll try to run down the fire escape. It'll be really, really icy. There's no way she'll be able to shoot and keep her balance at the same time—"

"It's too risky." This time he grabbed her arm. "That woman just shot a hole through your door."

"And another in my bedroom wall, I know. But if there's even a chance she really is the woman who robbed my uncle and aunt six years ago, there's no way I'm going to let her just run away again without a fight. Either way, she's the only hope we have right now of finding out why Kodiak attacked me at the barn or why Charlotte's former boyfriend would send anyone here looking for her. Please, Benjamin, we have to stop her."

She was standing there, barefoot, in a T-shirt and track pants, looking more like a college kid than the twenty-six-year-old woman he knew her to be.

He knew she was right. If he was alone, he'd chase after the intruder in a heartbeat. But he didn't want Piper to get hurt.

But it looked as if Piper was going after the masked blonde one way or the other. Short of physically picking her up and locking her in a closet he didn't expect he could stop her.

"How about this?" Piper said. "You head up into the attic and see if you can catch her before she makes it down the fire escape. I'll run outside through the garage and see if I can catch her coming the other way."

"Fine." He looked down at the thin gray T-shirt, track pants and slippers he wore. He wasn't exactly dressed to be chasing anyone around outside in freezing rain.

From above he heard the dog yip. At least Harry was okay. Then Harry yipped again. More insistent this time.

Piper squeezed his arm. "The dog—"

"What?" He looked up the stairs. "Oh."

Harry was holding a handgun in his mouth.

FIVE

Benjamin's jaw dropped. Had the intruder grown so desperate she'd thrown the gun at the dog? Or had the dog somehow disarmed her? Either way, the husky was now holding the weapon, gingerly but firmly upside down by the handle. If the situation wasn't so dangerous, he'd have laughed.

"I've got to go get that. You stay safe, okay? Just because she's lost her gun doesn't mean she's not dangerous."

"You, too." Piper squeezed his arm, then she took off running barefoot down the stairs.

Harry was sitting now, gun still in his jaws, and his tail was wagging. Benjamin started up the loft stairs slowly, his hands raised. "Good dog. Give that to me. Careful. Okay?"

The dog set the gun down right between his paws, then he stepped back and waited for Benjamin.

"You are the best dog ever, you know that?" His eyes scanned the room. It was empty. He picked up the gun and slipped it into his pocket.

The sound of footsteps clattering on the fire escape drew his attention to the open window. He glanced out to see the blonde trying to break into a second-story window. "Hey! Stop!"

She glanced up, then pelted down the stairs.

He squeezed through the window and out into the storm. Freezing rain beat against his body. Cold metal stung his bare palms. His slippers pounded hard down the metal steps.

The blonde hit the ground and took off running through the ice-covered snow. Benjamin vaulted over the railing, catching her by the shoulder as they fell to the ground. The blonde kicked back frantically with both legs, and one lucky shot made contact with Benjamin's jaw, just hard enough to make his numb hands loosen their grasp.

She slipped from his hands and kept running.

His hand reached for the gun. No, surely he could catch her on foot without taking the risk of seriously hurting or even killing her.

Benjamin ran after her into the woods. Hail pelted his bare skin like rocks. His slippers were swallowed up in slush. The motion sensor lights flickered on in the forest ahead. She could run all she wanted, but the trees were lighting up around her like Christmas. Benjamin's legs ached. Thick branches heavy with snow pushed up against his body. His feet were bare now and numb.

A loud, guttural roar filled the air. He looked up just in time to see a bright light flying toward him. He leaped to the side. A neon yellow snowmobile swerved wildly through the trees, nearly knocking him over. Then it was gone.

He dropped to his knees as a groan filled his chest and left his lungs.

His fists hit the snow.

"Lord, was I wrong to show mercy?"

Yes, the woman had broken into Piper's room. But it seemed she was just a young, scared thing trapped in something she didn't understand. Under the circumstances he couldn't have guaranteed a nonlethal shot and even then he'd seen firsthand the damage bullets could do. He could no more ruthlessly shoot her— without at least trying to stop her in a more merciful way—than he could shoot a frightened animal.

Not that wild animals weren't lethal when spooked.

"Benjamin!" Piper was running toward him.

She had boots on her feet and a huge black cape enveloping her head. A new hockey stick was clutched in one hand. Harry trailed behind her, protective and alert.

She looked fierce. She looked vulnerable.

She was breathtaking.

There was something clunky slung around her neck. An unexpectedly hard heartbeat knocked his chest. His boots. She'd tied the laces together and tossed them around her before running out. She pulled his boots off over her head and handed them to him. There was a pair of oversize hockey socks stuffed inside one them. Not his, but they'd fit. His fingers brushed the back of her hand. "Thank you."

"No problem."

He paused for a moment, once again feeling the urge to hug her and not knowing how she'd take it. It was funny. Surely he was practically an expert on offering comforting hugs by now—between hugging his sister, his friends, people at church and even clients who needed that bit of extra encouragement to try some extreme sport they'd never done before. Yet whenever he was around Piper he was suddenly awkward about it.

He knelt down and put his boots on. "I'm sorry. She got away. I thought I had her for a moment but she had a snowmobile."

"Yellow with flame stickers? A neighbor reported it stolen this morning."

"That's the one." He tied up the laces. Something warm and heavy fell unexpected around his shoulders. He stood carefully.

Piper had thrown her large wool cape around him so that now it enveloped them both. Then she slipped both hands around his waist and gave him a firm, strong squeeze. "Don't beat yourself up, Benjamin. She had both a head start and a snowmobile. Now, come on, let's get somewhere warm."

She stepped back and slipped beside him again, holding her edge of the cloak with one hand. Conflicting thoughts flooded his mind, blocking his ability to think. She'd have been able to run so much faster if she hadn't stopped to grab his boots, let alone a pair of socks. And she'd have been so much more nimble if she'd just grabbed her ski jacket, instead of an oversize cloak that was large enough to cover them both. *She won't let me take care of her. Yet here she is taking care of me.*

"Just don't freeze, okay?" Piper added. "You can't be in a wedding on Christmas Eve or on an airplane Christmas night if you've got hypothermia and frostbite."

"Thank you." His voice sounded as if it was coming from somewhere deep inside his chest. He turned to look at her. She was standing so close that if he tilted his head down just an inch or two he'd be kissing her on the nose. He had to stop that line of thinking. "Hopefully, the mechanic will have my truck back on the road before lunchtime."

She nodded slowly. "I just hope that when we get back to the house, the police will be waiting for us."

But before they could start back, the lights went out, plunging them and the forest into darkness.

In a heartbeat the forest was so dark she could no longer see Benjamin's face hovering just beside hers. The world fell silent, except for the beating of ice pellets on the trees.

"Did the motion-sensor lights go off?" he asked.

She could feel the cloak shake as he waved his hand around to reactivate them.

"They shouldn't, no. They're on a very long timer." She pulled away from him and from the protection of the cloak. Then she waved both hands above her head. The world stayed dark. She glanced through the trees but saw only darkness. "We should also be able to see the house lights from here, but I can't see them, either. The bad weather must've caused a short in the electrical circuit somewhere."

"I'm sure it'll be okay." Benjamin's arm landed on her shoulders, warm, soft and strong. "Do you have a backup generator?"

"Yeah. It's in a shed by the garage. But it should have kicked in if the main power went out." She frowned. They started walking as she talked. "Hopefully it's just another quick power glitch. Fortunately, there's a fireplace for warmth, the stove is gas and I've got plenty of battery-operated flashlights and lanterns."

Benjamin kept pace beside her. She was in the crook of his shoulder now, with his arm holding the cape around her shoulder. His hand rested lightly on her forearm. A moment ago she'd hugged him without stopping to think. Now, in the darkness, the simple gesture of his hand on her arm somehow felt like more than she was ready for. But a part of her was grateful for the warmth he provided. Even through her gloves and cloak she could feel the cold and damp seeping through. Cold air and freezing rain stung her face. The dog slipped under the cloak between them. On this cold, wet night they all needed to stay warm. Even the dog knew that.

"I wish I knew if Blondie was Charlotte." Slowly her eyes adjusted to the dark winter night. "But she was wearing a mask and trying to disguise her voice. Not to mention it's been six years since Charlotte crashed through here like a tornado."

"I'm not sure I'm clear on what happened between you and her back then," Benjamin said.

Fair enough. For that matter neither was she.

"I did most of my college by correspondence, so I could be here to help my uncle and aunt. When I was twenty, I did one semester in Ottawa to finish up my degree. Charlotte had a two-bedroom apartment and had listed a room for rent online. I'd hoped we'd become friends, but we really weren't. She was the kind of person who kept to herself and never made eye contact. Her life revolved around her history degree and her boyfriend, Alpha. Sometimes I'd catch bruises on her arms and I wondered if he was hurting her. But she wouldn't talk to me. I was always planning on moving out at Christmas and coming home. So, I was really surprised when she asked if she could come here for the holidays."

She glanced at the dark sky above. A flurry of falling ice filled her eyes. "She was on her phone with Alpha the whole car ride here. Sounded like he was yelling at her. We arrived and went to a church party with my old youth group. I barely saw her over the next couple of days. She kept slipping out and going places. I'd wake up in the night and her bed would be empty. Uncle Des just told me that he caught her kissing someone in the woods and chased the guy off. Described him as young, tall and broad-shouldered. I assume it was Alpha. I guess Alpha's in his late twenties now. While there are a whole lot of things about this whole Charlotte-Alpha-Kodiak-Blondie situation that I don't know, I am convinced that Blondie knows Alpha. You should have seen her panicked reaction when I mentioned his name. She's terrified of him."

Which could mean Blondie was Charlotte and the man with the bear tattoo was Alpha. Except that Blondie didn't react at all when Piper had asked her about a man with a bear tattoo. She closed her eyes for a moment and listened to the storm pushing through the trees. Just when she thought the terrifying picture of what had happened these past few hours was swimming into some kind of focus, everything stopped making sense again.

Their footsteps crunched through the snow. Benjamin's arm tightened around her shoulder. "You said she robbed you?"

"She did, Christmas Eve." Piper opened her eyes. "While we were all down in the barn, singing carols and eating potluck, she snuck through the woods to The Downs and trashed the place."

"When you say trashed the place—"

"She went through every room and all the guests' things looking for stuff to steal. She ripped open presents. She knocked our Christmas tree through the front window and even smashed the nativity my aunt had on the fireplace mantel."

They stepped out from under the shelter of the tree canopy into the storm, which seemed to have intensified. Benjamin pulled the cloak over their heads as they jogged to a small shed behind the garage. The shed was windowless, smelled like gasoline and was every bit as cold as the outside air. Harry slipped in ahead of them and curled up by the wall. Piper slipped out from under the cloak and let its full weight fall on Benjamin.

"We never had a lot of money." She set down the hockey stick and reached for a small battery-powered lamp hanging just inside the door. "So almost all the decorations she destroyed were homemade, mostly by me, including the nativity she broke into bits. A lot of the handmade garlands she ripped into pieces I'd made when I was five or six. The star on the top of the tree was something I'd made out of vintage newspaper when I was about eight, and I couldn't even find it in the wreckage. It was all too mean and petty for words."

She ran her hand over her face. *And I'm not even telling you the part about how she, or an accomplice, hit me over the head, knocked me out and locked me in the kindling box. Because even the memory of that makes me feel too pathetic and vulnerable for words.*

Holding out the lantern, she made her way over to the generator that sat in the corner, silent and cold. She bent down beside it, pushed the button and held it. It didn't start.

"I'm sorry. It must have been pretty hard to forgive her for all that." Benjamin's voice floated behind her in the darkness.

Was it even possible to forgive someone who'd never come back to ask for forgiveness?

She looked back up at Benjamin. "The generator's not working. Any suggestions?"

"If it's a motor problem I might be able to fix it. I've tinkered around with a lot of boat motors and vehicle engines." He moved passed her and knelt by her feet. He reached up, took her hand and moved the light over the generator. "Just hold that there, please, and don't move."

Thick snow dotted his hair and beard. His eyes were gray-blue in the lamplight. Oddly, she hadn't noticed the gray in them last summer. When he'd been standing outside waiting for her that last night on the dock by the pavilion, his eyes had seemed as dark and fathomless as the water spreading out behind him.

"Don't ever marry a sweetheart until you've both summered and wintered your romance..." Something Aunt Cass had said flickered in the back of her mind. It had been her aunt's way of trying to explain in the gentlest way possible why Piper's mother's whirlwind marriages never seemed to work.

But why was she remembering that now? She had no future with Benjamin. He wasn't her sweetheart and this wasn't a romance. He was just a friend and would be leaving as soon as his truck was repaired.

Benjamin muttered something under his breath. He stood.

"I'm sorry, Piper." His hands brushed her shoulders. "But it looks like someone sabotaged your generator."

SIX

"Sabotage?" Piper's body was shaking. She couldn't tell if it was from cold, anger or shock.

In an instant, Benjamin had wrapped the cloak back around her shoulders.

"I'm sorry," he said. "Looks like somebody cut the fuel line. Probably why it smells like gas in here."

Her mouth opened but no words came out.

"And I think somebody stole your gasoline," he added. "It's hard to see in the dark, but the tank looks nearly empty. Thankfully, the police are already on their way and we can pick up a new generator tomorrow."

He was right. There was hardly anything she could do about the situation in the middle of the night. But right now, it just felt like one problem more than she was able to manage. She hung the lantern back on the hook by the door but she didn't switch it off. Light glowed in the tiny wooden room, sending shadows shifting back and forth across the floor and up the walls. Snow flew in the doorway toward them in a wild frenzy. She knew she should head back to the house, but her legs felt too tired to move.

"Piper?" Benjamin's voice dropped. "It's going to

be okay. I promise. Before I leave tomorrow, I'm going to help you. My truck won't be fixed until lunchtime at least. Until then, I'm all yours, whatever you need."

I'm all yours. It was a common enough turn of phrase she'd heard dozens of times from people who'd offered to lend a spare pair of hands. *"You need a baker? You need furniture moved? You just tell me what you need. I'm all yours."* But somehow, hearing it from Benjamin's mouth right now turned her jaw tighter, like when the dentist used to tighten her childhood braces. Benjamin was there for her, for a brief, limited time, as the kind of friend who chased off intruders and helped with small engine repair. Nothing more.

His arms opened as he stepped toward her and she could practically feel the warmth of his chest, just inches away from hers. Did he think she didn't notice the support he was offering? Did he have any idea how hard she was fighting the urge to just fall into his arms? He was being a supportive friend and a friend was what she needed. But if she let herself hug him tonight, the simple touch of his hand could once again set her foolish heart up for failure.

"We might have a portable backup generator," she said. "I'll have to ask my uncle where he put it. We only got a permanent one installed a few years ago, after Charlotte—" Sudden tears rushed to her eyes—tears of frustration, exasperation, exhaustion. She blinked hard but still they flooded her voice. "After Charlotte robbed us. The lights on the path wouldn't light up that night. But Aunt Cass rallied. She called everyone and asked them to bring flashlights and lanterns, and we paraded through the trees to the barn in one long, glorious, beautiful line."

Piper should have stayed with them in the warm barn, drinking hot apple cider and singing songs about how God touched the earth on Christmas. But instead, when she'd realized Charlotte was missing, she'd grabbed a flashlight and slipped out. The lights had been off at the house. There'd been a swift, hard, painful blow to the head—and she'd woken up alone, terrified and locked in the kindling box beside the woodpile.

The shed door blew shut, cutting off the morbid memory. The lamp fell from the hook, casting shadows at their feet. Her lip quivered. It wasn't fair how the memories came back to disturb her every Christmas no matter how hard she worked to undo the damage she'd done in trusting Charlotte. Now Charlotte might be back and whatever she'd gotten herself into this time, she was bringing even more chaos, not to mention danger, to The Downs.

"Hey." Benjamin's hands touched her shoulders. "It's okay."

"No, it's not." She'd said the words under her breath, but still he'd managed to hear them.

"Yeah, it is." He looked into her eyes with that same soulful look he'd given her so many times back on the island. It was a look that said she could trust him. It was a look she'd been so certain meant he was every bit as drawn to her as she was to him. "Or at least, it's going to be. You're strong, Piper, and you're going to get through this. But even the strongest person alive is allowed to fall apart sometimes. So, if you want a comforting hug, or a shoulder to cry on, or even a sparring partner to box a couple of rounds with until the world feels saner, I'm here for you, okay?"

He stepped closer, never breaking eye contact. His

hand brushed lightly along her hair, as if he was almost afraid of touching her. Back on the island last summer, they'd jostled and play-fought like pals. Now, though, they both seemed uncertain about touching each other. Slowly, tentatively, his hands slid down her back until they reached her waist. Something pricked deep inside her chest, like a lure slipping inside her rib cage and pulling her toward him.

His breath brushed against her face. "If my flight wasn't nonrefundable and if I didn't have that charity sailing voyage, I'd stay a bit longer, as long as you needed me around to get things back on track."

How long would that have been, exactly? Until Charlotte and whoever was after her were caught? Until the renovations were done and her uncle and aunt moved back in? All the while, he'd be pacing the wooden floors like a mountain lion desperate to run.

The shed door flew open with a bang, a second before the cold wind rushed in. A light flashed across their faces and they leaped apart.

"There you are!" Gavin stood in the doorway, knee-deep in the snow and shivering in a shiny ski jacket that was very stylish but way too thin. He clutched the industrial-sized flashlight she kept hanging beside the stairs for emergencies. "The power is out. The cell towers are out. That ramshackle bed-and-breakfast of yours is so cold my poor Trisha can't sleep. You do know she's pregnant?"

Yes, she'd barely seen the heavyset brunette since they'd moved in, but Gavin kept reminding her. Guilt filled her heart. Her guests had actually come tramping out in the snow looking for her—and found her in a shed, a breath away from falling into Benjamin's arms.

"Young lady, the police are here." Tobias appeared in the doorway behind Gavin, a long plaid scarf wound several times around his face. "They say they wish to speak to you regarding the incidents tonight. I trust that you're taking all this seriously."

"Yes, I'm taking it very seriously." She wrapped the cloak around herself picked up the hockey stick she'd brought for protection and started for the house, the two guests, Benjamin and the dog following behind her. She felt guilty for leaving Benjamin without the shelter of the cloak. But somehow she felt uncomfortable about the idea of sharing it with him now, too, and knew there was no way Benjamin would take it all for himself. Fortunately the house was only twenty feet away and Benjamin was able to run it in fifteen paces. She probably should have just grabbed two coats to begin with and not brought the hockey stick, but it was the quickest makeshift weapon she'd been able to find. But this wasn't a game. Charlotte's own unique brand of chaos was back. Only this time, Piper wasn't a frightened, trapped girl waiting to be rescued.

She stepped into The Downs's garage. Warmth filled her body and steam covered her glasses. She slid her glasses up onto the top of her head and stomped the snow off her boots. "I'm sorry, I didn't realize the police had arrived. I didn't see a car."

"They're in the living room with Trisha," Gavin said through chattering teeth. "They skied here, because the roads are bad and the salters aren't out yet. What kind of town is it where the cops can't keep their own roads open?"

A small town, she silently replied, *with only a few hundred people, in a place where the roads got really icy.*

"I'm sure they'll be open by morning." Piper grabbed a towel off a rack by the door, dried her glasses, then dropped to her knees and quickly ran it over Harry's snow-caked fur. "These things take time."

"The former mayor of Toronto experienced much derision for calling out the military to clear the snow one year." Tobias unwound his scarf. "But there is something to be said for military efficiency. Even the British troops were efficient enough during the eighteen hundreds to prime, load and fire at least three musket rounds in under a minute."

She would have laughed, if she hadn't suspected the tactics author wasn't actually trying to be funny. She stood up and started toward the kitchen door. "That's interesting."

A heavy hand landed on her shoulder. She turned. Tobias leaned in toward her, his pale eyes focused intensely on her face. "I do want to assure you that if there's anything I can do, please don't hesitate to ask. I know how much the pressure of your college studies must be weighing on you, and I have studied extensively about how ordinary human beings react to extraordinary pressures in times of crisis."

"That's kind of you." She forced a smile. "But thankfully my college days are long behind me."

Though apparently the shadow they'd cast still lingered.

"There are cops in the living room." A young woman with short brown hair stood in the kitchen doorway. Trisha's narrow face was so pale it was almost white. A huge bulky sweatshirt swamped her form. Her arms cradled a very round stomach.

"Trisha!" Gavin ran over to her and threw his arm

around her. "What are you doing out here? You should be in bed!"

Her red, puffy eyes glanced around the room. Trisha's voice was so soft and timid it was barely more than a whisper. "How long until the power comes back on?"

"Yeah." Gavin's voice rose. "How much longer will be the power be out? Because if it's much longer, we will be looking for a new hotel and expecting you to refund our stay."

Piper wouldn't blame them if they did. She closed her eyes, then drew in a deep breath and let it out again as she silently prayed. *Lord, it's the middle of the night. I'm exhausted. I'm overwhelmed. But as much as I need money to renovate The Downs, these people came here looking for a safe place to stay.*

"I'm afraid I'm going to have to close The Downs, at least for the next few days." She forced herself to say the words first. Then she opened her eyes.

Trisha's gaze dropped to the floor, Gavin gasped as if she'd just stolen his air and Tobias started to argue. She held up her hand and kept talking too quickly for them to get a word in. "I'll still be going ahead with the Christmas Eve event in the barn, and you'll all be welcome to come for that. But I have no choice but to close the bed-and-breakfast to guests. There've been two different armed trespassers on the property in the past few hours, the power is out and the weather is freezing. I will find you new rooms at good hotels in the morning, reimburse your stay and cover any financial difference. Again, I'm sorry."

"Sorry's not good enough." Gavin let go of Trisha and stormed toward her. He stepped in so close she could almost taste the stale smell of liquor on his breath.

His finger jabbed toward her face. "Do you have any idea the inconvenience you've put us through?"

Did he have any idea what she was dealing with? All he had to do was change hotels.

Tobias took Trisha by the arm and steered her back into the kitchen.

Piper crossed her arms and faced Gavin's glare. "Again, I apologize. But there's only so much I can do."

"Oh, there's plenty you can and will do to make this right." Gavin snorted. "You think I didn't do my homework? You think I don't know there's not another decent hotel within half an hour's drive of here?"

"Hey, man, back off and give her some space, all right?" Benjamin calmly but firmly stepped between them. His hand brushed Gavin's arm. "She's doing the best she can."

And she was also capable of fighting her own battles and of hollering for the cops in the living room if she felt threatened. She wouldn't hide behind Benjamin now. Gavin was right about the lack of good hotels in the area, especially ones that offered full suites like The Downs. Depending on how long it took her to find her guests vacancies at this time of year, Benjamin might end up hitting the road before they did.

"Don't touch me." Gavin stepped back, his eyes darting from Benjamin to Piper. "I'll sue you. And I'll press charges for assault if he dares lay a hand on me again. Trisha and I own a successful law firm in Ottawa, and you can't afford the legal bill of making us unhappy. I saw that newspaper article last fall. I know you're saving up for some major renovation, with a ground-floor suite for some disabled relative. You can't afford the lawsuit we'll drop on you. You can't afford to make an enemy of me. Because we don't even need to win to ruin you."

A cold, threatening smirk crossed the young man's lips. But she didn't break his gaze.

"I'm sorry you feel that way. Now, I'm going to go talk to the police. Tomorrow morning I'll serve breakfast and then do my best to find you and your wife a suite somewhere suitable, especially as Trisha doesn't seem well. Then I'll expect you to pack up and kindly get out of The Downs."

The morning sun woke Benjamin. It was bright, glaring and shining down on him through the huge, towering windows of The Downs living room. He threw one arm over his eyes and stretched his legs, feeling for the large mass of heavy dog he'd gotten used to feeling curled up on his feet.

No dog. Then he remembered. After helping Piper replace her door with the one that had been on an upstairs linen closet, he'd insisted Harry bunk in Piper's room. After the police had taken statements and Blondie's gun, the rest of The Downs's residents had gone up to bed. But Benjamin had fallen asleep on the couch, fully clothed and with a full view of the entire second-floor landing, the front door and the front and back windows. All the bedroom doors were still closed. He reached for the lamp on the end table behind him and barely managing to stop himself from slipping off the narrow couch and landing on the floor.

He flicked the switch. Nothing happened.

The Downs was still without power.

The old grandfather clock in the corner of the living room said it was a quarter to nine. So, he'd had five hours of sleep, then. Well, he'd survived before on less. Soon enough, he'd be living full-time on a sailboat and would have to get used to grabbing sleep when he could.

A smile crossed his lips. Tomorrow was Christmas Eve. Only two days left until he got on that plane and left the bitter cold of Canada behind for the glorious heat of an Australian summer. Of course, he should really trim his beard before his sister's wedding rehearsal tonight, not to mention get a haircut, too. Before that, he'd need to collect his truck. And say goodbye to Piper.

Through the window he could see a thin layer of ice coating the world outside. Dazzling blue sky peeked through the glistening branches. *Lord, there's so much more I wish I could do to help Piper before I go. Help me do the best I can, in the short time I have left.* That was a good prayer and one that made him feel better. He'd never be able to solve everything and it never hurt to remind himself of that. But there was always something he could fix.

Starting with coffee.

He threw a couple of extra logs into the fireplace then walked into the kitchen. No power meant no coffeemaker. But the burner on the gas stove turned on without a hitch and a quick rummage in the cupboard beside the sink turned up a couple of solid pots plus a large skillet. There was a loaf of fresh thick bread in the bread box, real maple syrup in the walk-in pantry, and butter and a carton of eggs in the fridge, which was still fairly cold. He piled his finds on the counter and started a pot of water boiling for coffee. Wouldn't be much of an outdoorsman if he didn't know how to brew a decent cup over an open flame and this morning, campfire coffee would have to do. He ground some coffee with a mortar and pestle, and then added it to the boiling water. A blob of butter went into the hot skillet on the stove. He'd just started whistling when he heard noise behind him.

"Where's Piper?" Gavin stood behind him, scowling.

Benjamin wondered what had brought him and Trisha to book their holidays at The Downs, anyway? As much as Gavin had protested about moving out, neither of them seemed happy staying here, either.

A warm smile crossed Benjamin's face, learned by years of customer service. "Good morning. I'm not quite sure where she is. But there's some fresh coffee brewing if you'd like a mug. Did you sleep well?"

The young man snorted. "The power's still out."

"Well, then it's a good thing you and Trisha will be moving to a new hotel."

Gavin's forehead furrowed. Benjamin had seen that same overly worried look before. Usually on the face of someone who was thinking twice about his decision to book a tandem leap after the plane had reached altitude and a parachute was already strapped to his back. Not from someone about to be asked whether they'd prefer milk or sugar. Benjamin's gaze ran from the man's overly styled hair down to his designer boots. If he had to guess, he'd peg Gavin as someone who'd come from the expectation of money, but actually lacked a decent jingle in his pocket.

Gavin's eyes narrowed in return as if he didn't appreciate the appraisal. "Tobias said your last name was Duff. Are you the same Benji Duff who nearly killed himself because he didn't know how to drive a motorbike? We had to watch some stupid documentary about you every single winter in school assembly, from like grade seven onward."

Benjamin remembered when one of the national television current-affairs shows had done a sensational hatchet job, heavy on the scare tactics. Schools loved it.

"That's me," he said, "but it was a snowmobile accident actually. And the friend I was riding with died. His name was Chris." He turned his back on Gavin, cracked eight eggs in a bowl and whisked them until they were frothy.

"Gavin, my good man! Good morning! How did your wife sleep?" Tobias's voice boomed through the doorway. "I do hope the fact breakfast is late isn't a sign some tragedy has befallen poor Piper."

Did he mean some new tragedy besides everything that happened yesterday? Benjamin gritted his teeth. He didn't know how Piper did it. Sure, as a sports instructor he'd dealt with his share of difficult people. But not the self-centered kinds like these.

"Trisha isn't feeling well this morning," Gavin said. "Headache."

Which considering whom she was married to wasn't a surprise.

Tobias clicked his teeth. "Well, it's no wonder. Studying for a university degree can be very stressful on a young woman, not to mention quite expensive."

Pregnant, a lawyer, studying for a university degree and married to Gavin? Yeah, that would be more than enough for anyone. Benjamin tuned the conversation out, slid a large knife from the cutting board and sliced the bread in quick, even strokes.

"What university do you attend, young man?" Tobias hovered over Benjamin's shoulder. He couldn't help but notice the older man had shown up for breakfast in a tweed jacket, bow tie and fedora.

"I never went to university." Benjamin dipped the slices of bread in the eggs and laid them in the skillet. "I was a lifeguard and camp counselor as a teenager, then went straight into working for a sports store after high school, while taking some business courses by correspondence." He flipped the bread. It was golden brown. "Opened my own business when I was twenty-three."

Tobias sighed pityingly. He laid one hand on Benjamin's shoulder and leaned in as if delivering terminally bad news. "Well, not everyone has what it takes to handle academia."

"Guess not," Benjamin said. He dropped the piece of French toast onto a plate, just barely managing to keep from swatting the pompous older man with the spatula. "I mean, getting offered a full scholarship to both McGill and the University of British Columbia because of my straight A average was sweet. But my sister was dealing with some personal stuff and I didn't want to leave her. Now, if you want to have a seat at the dining-room table, I'll be out with a pot of coffee in a second." Benjamin pushed the jug of maple syrup into older man's hands and handed the younger one a fistful of cutlery. Then he turned back to the stove.

"Benji's unflappable!" his big sister, Meg, liked to say, as if being steady was some magical power he possessed, instead of a side effect of growing up with an anxious sister, a distant father with a heart condition and a hysterical mother. Someone had needed to bring some calm into that house. Besides, why get all flapped up about something as minor as somebody else's bad attitude? There were already too many things in life you couldn't control and only a few that actually mattered.

Once breakfast was made and served, Gavin took some up to Trisha in her room, and then sat with Tobias who cheerfully showed off what looked like a replica World War I hand grenade that the author wore on a loop on his belt. It was almost ten by the time Benjamin was alone again. He hadn't seen Piper yet. But last summer it had been pretty clear she wasn't really much of a morning person.

His cell phone rang. It was his sister, Meg. Also, he'd apparently missed a call from the mechanic. "Hello?"

"Benji! How are you? I got your message about last night. Where are you?" His sister spoke so quickly her voice was almost breathless.

The familiar gnawing of guilt filled his gut immediately. Meg might be four years older than him. But she was also a tiny slip of a thing who'd been fighting an anxiety disorder for years. She was on the verge of getting married and he was still a seven-hour's drive away.

"I'm so sorry, sis. I'm still at The Downs." He ran his hands down his jeans. "Just finished making the guests French toast and coffee. You'd be impressed. I used a mortar and pestle and everything. Even added some cinnamon. Or nutmeg. Not sure which. Piper doesn't exactly label her spices."

There was a slight pause on the other end of the phone. "Where's Piper?"

"I don't know. Thought I'd let her sleep in. Haven't seen Harry yet and the two of them are sharing a room." He ran his hand over the back of his neck. "But I promise, I'll do everything in my power to be at the rehearsal tonight."

"Whatever you do, don't leave too late. There's a wickedly heavy snowstorm scheduled to come in later tonight that could cause all types of chaos on the roads. They're already pretty terrible as it is. Black ice, strong winds, accidents everywhere. If anything goes wrong, call me. There's still something major we need to talk about. It's kind of important, but I'd rather do it in person and it can wait for tonight."

"Don't worry. My truck has four-wheel drive and really great snow tires. There's nothing better I could be driving. I'll take it really slow and drive safely, I promise."

After another long pause on the other end of the line he was sure something was wrong. He and his sister had shared a house and each other's lives ever since their parents had moved to Florida years ago. He could read trouble in her silences at a dozen paces. *Please, Lord, protect her from having another panic attack. Not over this. Not because of me.* "Look, sis. I know you're worried, but it's going to be okay. You've got a great man by your side and people who love you—"

A laugh echoed down the line. Gentle. Genuine. "No, no, bro, I'm fine! I'm better than fine. I'm really excited about getting married tomorrow. *You* are the one I'm worried for right now."

"Me?" Benjamin blinked. "What? Why? I'm just fine…"

"Are you sure? You're standing in Piper's kitchen, making breakfast—"

"Because this is a bed-and-breakfast. I'm just being a good friend."

Last summer his sister had totally misread his friendship with Piper. He could still picture the way Meg had looked up at him over her coffee mug and said, "You really like Piper. I do, too. Just be careful there, okay? Don't hand your heart away to someone here if you're planning on heading overseas. I'd hate to see either of you get hurt." He'd already caused more than enough hurt to the people he loved, enough to last a lifetime. That very night when he and Piper had gone out to dinner he'd explained to her, in no uncertain terms, that he'd decided he'd never have the kind of close relationship with anyone where they'd be relying on him for their security or happiness, including a wife or family of his own.

Still, when he'd first told Meg that he'd asked Piper to give his dog a good home, he'd gotten a whole new warning for his troubles.

Looked as if he was in for round three.

"You got a call this morning from your friend in Brighton," Meg added. "He's flying out from England to Australia on the twenty-sixth to join your sailing team. Also, the final payment went through on the boat—"

"Wonderful. Honestly, Meg, I can't wait to hop on that plane Christmas night. Stop worrying, okay? I've been waiting and saving all my life for this. I'm not about to let the dream go now. Not for anything—"

"But, Benjamin, are you sure?"

He opened his mouth to argue. Then shut it again. His sister was so concerned she'd actually called him Benjamin—not Benji, bro, or any number of the other things she called him from time to time. He gripped the counter with both hands. "I don't get it, sis. Why are you being like this? You've never once given me grief about a woman before."

"I've never seen you look at anyone or talk about

anyone the way you do with Piper. This boat, this adventure, is all you've ever wanted. You put your dream on hold for me for years, didn't you? And now, I don't know what to think. I'd hate to see you give up your boat. But at the same time, I know someone like Piper doesn't come along that often in a lifetime, and if being with her at that bed-and-breakfast had even a chance of making you happy—"

"Meg, listen to me." He was so frustrated with her for inventing a concern like this, especially when she already had more than enough to worry about. Sure, he was attracted to Piper as a person, as a friend. And sure, she was more than a little easy on the eyes. But just because he recognized and admired who she was didn't mean it was a romantic attraction. Certainly nothing so deep that it would threaten the course of either of their lives. "I promise you, there is no way I see this bed-and-breakfast playing any kind of role in my future. Yes, I spent years living on the island, because I loved you and you needed me. But you're my *sister*. Plus, living there allowed me to build an amazing, successful sports business on the biggest freshwater island in the world. I know where I'm going. No pair of pretty dark eyes is ever going to make me give up a dream I really care about to hang out in a stodgy, boring old bed-and-breakfast in a tiny little town, making miserable people eggs and coffee. Being trapped here does not and will not make me happy. I'd rather move back into your basement."

There was a crash behind him. He turned.

Piper stood in the doorway.

Bright sun cascaded down her wet hair and illuminated her cheekbones. Deep eyes fringed with long dark lashes met his. Shivers ran down his arms, so powerfully that his heart leaped a beat. *Okay, so maybe there is a little bit of an attraction.*

And judging by the hurt in her eyes and the broken dishes scattered by her feet, she'd heard every thoughtless word he'd just said.

SEVEN

Benjamin spun toward her. One hand clutched a phone to his ear and the other hand waved through the air as if trying to erase the words that had just flown out of his mouth. But it was too late. She'd heard them. What's more, she believed them.

There was no way a man like Benjamin was ever going to be happy in a place like The Downs. It would be completely contrary to the adventurous, daring man that she knew. *Don't worry. I was never going to ask you to trade in your dream for me.* But she could've done without hearing him call her home a stodgy, boring old place for miserable people.

His eyes met hers for a second with a look so pained it almost bordered on panic. Then he turned back to his phone. "Meg, I've got to go. I'll give you a call once I get my truck. You, too. Bye."

She bent down and started picking up pieces of the broken dishes.

He bent down, too. "I'm sorry about that. I don't know how much you just heard. But I think I phrased something really badly. I definitely didn't mean to imply—"

"Don't worry about it." She stood quickly and dropped the pieces into the garbage. "I'm sorry. I didn't mean to eavesdrop."

Benjamin stood slowly and walked over to the stove. She grabbed some paper towels and wiped the floor where the dishes had landed.

"That was just my sister. She wanted to make sure I was still planning on being there for the rehearsal tonight. And apparently I missed a call from the garage."

"You should probably call them." She walked past him to the sink. "Thank you for making breakfast. That was very thoughtful of you."

"Well, yeah. Anything I can do to make things easier for you while I'm here."

"I know you're in a hurry to go." She ran both hands through her hair. It was still damp from the shower. "Just give me a few moments to make some phone calls. Then I'm going to walk into town to visit my uncle and aunt. If you don't mind waiting, I'll show you how to get to the garage."

"Great. I should really go get changed and pack." He started toward the living room, then paused. "Oh, and if you're going to have coffee from the saucepan skim it off the top. The grounds will have settled at the bottom. And I left a couple of slices of French toast in the oven."

"Thanks." She grabbed a bag of dog food from the pantry, then slipped past him to pour some in the bowl by the back door. It was amazing how much two people could move around such a tiny space without touching or even making eye contact.

She turned back. Benjamin was leaning in the kitchen doorway, one arm up against the lintel. His gaze seemed to sweep over her like an X-ray. "Is everything okay, Piper?"

Please, don't make me have this conversation.

She forced a smile across her lips and nodded. "Just give me a few minutes, and then we'll go get your truck."

While he went to pack his bag she pulled The Downs credit card out of her wallet and picked up the phone to book luxury hotel suites for her guests.

Forty minutes later, Piper sat on the front steps of The Downs. She looked down the road where Benjamin had gone to give Harry one final walk. Ice seemed to coat the whole world. A thin layer enveloped every twig, pine needle and stone like glass. Fresh snow danced from the sky. The great irony of winter was that the world kept getting more beautiful the more dangerous it became.

She twisted her hair behind her head and tied it into a knot. Finding new accommodations for her guests had been easier than expected. A high-priced spa near Niagara, with an indoor pool and gourmet buffet, had a couple of one-bedroom suites available on short notice at a steep markup. But considering the amount of eye rolling, complaining and protest it took to get the irritating lawyer, his withdrawn wife and the middle-aged author to take the very generous trade and leave, it almost made the money she'd be losing worth it just to have some peace.

Almost.

Between paying out refunds and booking the last-minute rooms at a higher cost, The Downs restoration fund had just lost over a thousand dollars.

Harry's wet, furry body bounded around the corner, followed by Benjamin at less than half the speed. "Careful. It's insanely slippery. I've already fallen down twice. They're all gone?"

"Yeah." She stood. "Wasn't easy. Gavin was still threatening to throw the full weight of their law firm behind suing us as they drove away. If he makes good on his threat there's no telling the damage he could do."

"I don't think you have to worry about that." Benjamin shook his head. "I'm pretty sure Gavin won't sue. In fact, I'm pretty sure I caught him out on a lie this morning. I didn't really put two and two together at first. But you know how he said that he and Trisha own a law firm? Well, he also told me that he had to sit through that horrid documentary about my accident, every winter in school, starting since grade seven. Well, I can tell you for a fact that documentary came out when I was eighteen. Which means he's only about twenty-five. He may very well have already passed the bar, but that's a bit young to have already built your own successful law firm."

But not too young to be Alpha though, she realized. But was Alpha brazen enough to book a room in the very hotel he was getting Blondie to break into?

"In fact, the more I think about it the less I think his bluster is anything you need to worry about," Benjamin added. "The lawsuit would be terrible publicity for a small firm. Also, for what it's worth, Tobias seemed to think that Trisha was still in university. But he thought both you and I were university students, too."

"Although, I'm not sure Tobias listens very well." She walked over to Harry and ran her hand through his fur. "It's like he's not all there. I could never tell if he was eccentric, self-absorbed or slightly off his rocker. At least it's one less thing I'll have to worry about now."

"Are you sure?" The tone of Benjamin's voice was so serious that her feet paused on the ice.

"Of course." Of all the heavy things weighing on her mind right now, the ramblings of an overweight, middle-aged author didn't even budge the needle. "Tobias should be settling into a beautiful suite in a rather expensive spa right now surrounded by all sorts of people happy to hear his rambling stories."

"Not him—Gavin." Concern filled the depths of his eyes. "As far as lies go, it's an odd one for Gavin to tell. I don't like coincidences and here you have a young man telling stories and throwing his weight around at the exact same time you've got people breaking in and threatening you. We still don't know what Kodiak and Blondie were even after. And might I add Gavin isn't too young to either be Alpha or to be mixed up in this some other way."

"You're right." What else could she say, exactly? "But Gavin doesn't have the right build to be either Kodiak or Blondie."

"Well, I don't like uncertainty." Benjamin's voice sounded so deep in this throat it was nearly a growl. "There's something seriously wrong going on here. We don't know exactly what, let alone why and you're altogether too casual about it. There has to be something we can do."

She shook her head and crossed her arms. Did he miss the fact she'd just shut down the bed-and-breakfast, kicked out her guests and lost a huge chunk of money? What did he expect her to do? Start crying, fall into his arms and stay curled up there until the danger disappeared? "There are things that I can do, and I am doing them. You have a truck to pick up and a wedding rehearsal to get to."

But now he'd picked up such a verbal steam it was as if he hadn't heard her. "You told me that your uncle saw Charlotte kissing someone in the woods the night before she robbed you. What did he say he looked like again?"

Why was he pushing this? She appreciated the effort, but this wasn't the kind of problem that could be solved in five minutes before he took off.

"Tall, broad shoulders, young." She opened the door and whistled for Harry to come inside. The dog raced in. "But while Gavin is definitely young and tall, I wouldn't consider him to have broad shoulders."

"Clothes can do a lot to disguise someone's build—"

A horn honked, cutting off his words. She looked up to see a small red hatchback inch off the road and down into her driveway. A dark-haired man with a dazzling smile waved one hand out the window. She recognized him immediately. The back of the car was so overflowing with boxes and bags it looked as if it was starting its own garage sale.

"Dominic!" She skidded down the driveway toward him. "What are you doing here? And what's going on in the back of your car?"

"Hey, Pips!" Dominic unfolded his six-foot frame from the driver's seat. "My mom packed up my stuff when I was working out west. These are the remains of my misspent youth. It was taking up too much space at my sister's, so I moved it out to the car." He paused only for a second before he went on. "Just saw your aunt when I was visiting my grandma. She told me about the problems you were having. Suggested I swing by and see if you needed a hand."

"Oh, she did, did she?" Why was she not surprised?

"Please, don't send me away, Pips." He slapped a gloved hand over his heart. "It's a nonstop noise machine over at my sister's. She has five little kids under the age of seven. Five! I love them more than life itself, but I'm not cut out for that much noise and chaos. I haven't had five minutes of quiet to myself to study, and the police exam is in three weeks."

She glanced back at the empty house. Yeah, having a big, strong man sitting in her living room deterring trespassers while she was visiting her uncle and aunt probably wasn't the worst idea. She reached into her pockets and handed him the keys. "Go ahead. There's a dog in there somewhere, too. His name is Harry."

Benjamin frowned slightly.

She took a step back. "Oh, I'm sorry, I should do introductions. Dominic Bravo meet Benjamin Duff."

Benjamin reached for Dominic's hand and shook it firmly. His eyes darted down to their hands for barely a second. "Nice to meet you."

"No way!" Dominic's smile grew wider. "Piper, you're friends with Benji Duff? *The* Benji Duff, the extreme sports guy from Manitoulin Island?"

"The one and only."

"Dude!" Dominic clasped Benjamin's arm firmly and slapped him on the back. "I heard you speak last year. Went and downloaded one of your talks after that. Even gave Pip's Uncle Des a copy. You were incredible!" Dominic crossed his arms and looked at Piper. "This guy is the absolute best. Made me realize I had to quit mucking about and get serious about my life.

Please tell me you're getting him to stick around and give a talk tomorrow night at your Christmas Eve shindig. I'll call around to all the neighboring youth groups. You will totally pack the place."

Pack the place? She was just barely hanging on to the hope she'd still be able to pull off a halfway decent carol night without worrying about pulling in extra mouths to feed.

"No, thank you." Benjamin held up a hand. "That's really kind, but I'm actually about to hit the road."

"Merry Christmas, then." Dominic gave him one more thump on the shoulder. "Give me a shout next time you're down this way."

"Won't be for a while, I'm afraid. I sold my business. Bought myself a boat. Real beauty. I'm picking it up in Australia the day after Christmas. Going to sail around the world for charity and then start up a charter business."

"Of course you are." Dominic chuckled. "Wow. Stuff like that is why *you* are the man."

The image of Benjamin's sundrenched boat floated in the back of Piper's mind as they slid down the sidewalk into town. Had there been that much joy in his eyes this summer when he'd first told her of his dreams to buy a boat? Or had she been too caught up in her own foolish fantasy of somehow shoehorning this big, strong, adventurous man into her tiny little life?

"How well do you know Dominic?" Benjamin asked. "I mean, you're sure he's a good guy? You can vouch for him?"

Was that why Benjamin was looking down during their handshake? He was trying to check Dominic's wrists for a bear tattoo?

"Yes, I'm sure Dominic is a good guy!" Her eyes rolled to the thick clouds now filling the sky above. "He's the guy who found me when—"

Her words froze in her mouth as Benjamin's eyebrow rose. "He found you when?"

When I was hit over the head and locked in the kindling box. Only I never told you about that.

"Listen to me," she said. "I've known Dominic since we were kids. We went to the same church. He was a year behind me in school. Yeah, he was always a bit awkward and got into a few scrapes as a kid. But he has a good heart. He'd do anything for his family. Anything."

"All right, then."

Did that mean he believed her? Or just that he was done arguing about it?

Well, there was nothing to stop Benjamin from contacting the police and telling them all his suspicions about Dominic, Gavin or anybody. In fact, she wouldn't be surprised if he did.

"Dominic treated you like some kind of celebrity," she said. "Do you get that a lot?"

He shrugged. "Sometimes. People tend to think they know me. Either because of the talks I've done or that awful documentary on winter safety that schools keep showing. Most people are curious more than anything. But there've been plenty, like Gavin this morning, who've been downright rude and practically mocked me about it."

They walked slowly. The sidewalk was unevenly shoveled and only a few of the stores had sanded. Her eyes ran over the old familiar buildings of her childhood. The small independent grocery store had been bought out by a chain franchise a few years ago. The gift-and-flower shop seemed to change ownership once a year or so. But most of the street was the same as it had been since she was younger. She'd been desperate to escape The Downs as a teenager thinking adventures and excitement lay somewhere else.

Was that why she was so bothered by Benjamin's dreams to travel the world and live a carefree life?

A man with shaggy blond hair was slouched in front of the town's one bar puffing on a cigarette. A dirty red tuque was pulled down low on his scarred face. She nodded at him as they passed. He didn't look up so they kept walking. This dingy bar was the closest thing the town had to danger or excitement. When she'd realized Charlotte had been sneaking out, it's where Piper thought she'd been going.

Benjamin waited until they'd passed the bar then started talking again.

"Three years ago, a friend of mine was starting this white-water rafting business. I wanted to come in as an investor. I was really excited about it." He ran one hand across his head and adjusted his tuque. "But the rest of the team took a vote and decided they didn't want me. They were afraid it might lead to bad publicity and unwanted attention. Thought it might tarnish what they were trying to do."

"You can't be serious!" An icy breath caught in her throat. "You're such an incredible person! You're so good at what you do!"

He stopped walking and looked at her square on. The smile faded from his face. "Thank you. But think of it from their perspective. Imagine you're running a small, financially strapped business, and there's some-

one on your staff who's capable of bringing all sorts of
unwanted drama and chaos through your door at any
moment. Stupid teenagers are going to crank call you
every single winter because that old documentary's running again. People are going to walk in and demand a
selfie with the guy, or tell you to fire him because he's
an example of everything that's wrong with the world.
Every time helmet laws, snowmobile licenses, or tragic
winter accidents are in the news—or the calendar rolls
around to the middle of February—you might wake up
to see a news camera outside."

Was he still talking about his friend's business? Or
hers?

No. As much as part of her would be willing to take
all that on if it meant being near Benjamin, she also
couldn't imagine bringing that much chaos into The
Downs. Her uncle and aunt deserved far better than that.

His blue eyes focused on hers. "See, I chose to see
my accident as a mantle. I accepted it and did my best
to turn it into something awesome. But that doesn't
mean it's easy or that I'd wish it on anyone. With my
sister getting married tomorrow, it's time to start a new
chapter in my life. I'm almost thirty-one, and I can't remember the last time I went two weeks without having
to talk to someone somewhere about that day. I'm really
looking forward to being where I can be anonymous,
far enough away from Ontario that people don't know
that story." He emitted a wry chuckle. "Also, I really,
really don't like snow."

She looked past him. They were steps away from the
mechanic's garage.

Guess this was where they said goodbye.

"Travel safe, Benjamin." She reached out to hug him.

But he took her shoulders and gently held her out at arm's length.

"Wait. There's something else I need to say." His eyes were still fixed on her face, with such a raw unrelenting gaze that it made her heart tighten in her chest. "I want you to be happy, Piper."

"I am happy."

"No, I don't think you are. I respect that you want to renovate The Downs for your uncle and aunt—although you still haven't told me the details of their health problems, so I don't quite understand why you're as stressed-out about that as you are. But I know a thing or two about existing versus living. The Piper I met this summer on the island was so very *alive*. You were so excited you practically sparkled. Now that light is gone."

"You're right. You don't know the whole situation with my uncle and aunt." She dug her heels into the slippery snow. "But anybody can be happy swimming and hiking or floating off into the sunset. Now I'm at work."

"But your whole life is your work. Christmas Eve is work. Your home is your work—"

"Because I'm helping my uncle and aunt keep their home and only source of income!" She heard her voice rise, despite the cold air rushing into her lungs. "What else am I supposed to do? Let them lose their only source of income while I travel the world? They have no retirement savings. Their only asset is The Downs and it's mortgaged. They took me in when my dad left and my mom had one foot out the door. I'm not going to abandon them now."

Benjamin ran his hand through his hair. "Look, I'm sorry, I'm saying this all wrong and I didn't want to say goodbye this way. I just think you should try to find a compromise between the life you want and the one you're currently trapped in."

Trapped. There that word was again. Life here, with her at The Downs, was just some trap to escape. Benjamin's words to his sister flickered in the back of her mind. *"Being trapped here does not and will not make me happy."*

The blond smoker pushed off the wall and started sauntering their way. She didn't recognize him, but she couldn't know everyone, even in a town this size. She looked back at Benjamin. This wasn't the kind of conversation she wanted to have on a public street in front of an audience.

Better this conversation ended right now, before either of them said anything they regretted.

"Thanks for caring so much about my happiness. Thank you for everything." She gave Benjamin a quick hug and her lips brushed his cheek. "Safe voyage and merry Christmas."

Then she slipped into the alleyway beside the mechanic shop and hurried along the back route to Silver Halls before Benjamin could follow.

Piper disappeared around the corner leaving the scent of maple and cinnamon in her wake.

Was that goodbye?

He stared at the empty patch of snowy air where the tenacious brunette had been standing just moments ago. All the while he'd been packing his bag and walking Harry, he'd been practicing this great goodbye speech in his head. Probably for the best he never got to give it. If he was honest, he'd have probably just rambled on far too much about what a wonderful person he thought she was.

He pushed open the door to the mechanic's shop.

A tall, smiling young man in grease-stained overalls looked up at him from behind the counter.

The smoking blond man brushed past him, so close their shoulders almost bumped. He glanced back to see the man disappear into the alley behind Piper.

Benjamin froze in the doorway, with one foot on either side of the threshold and his hand still on the knob. Every warning signal in the back of his skull was clanging.

Was that man following Piper?

"Mr. Duff." The mechanic wiped his hands on a cloth. "Your truck is all ready to go."

"Thank you. That's awesome. I'll be with you in just one moment." He stepped back outside onto the street and let the door close behind him. He hiked his hockey bag up onto his shoulder and started toward the alley.

Maybe he was overreacting. After all, lots of people probably used this alley as a shortcut. But if there was even a chance that man was trailing Piper...

I can't risk it.

He stepped into the narrow alley.

It was deserted.

Now what? Benjamin started down the empty alley feeling increasingly foolish with every step. He passed a closed metal door that he presumed led to the back of the mechanic's shop. A towering pile of garbage bags loomed out of a Dumpster ahead on his right. The air smelled like grease. Slush and motor oil mingled together under his boots. Up ahead he noticed boxy letters spelled out what looked like Silver Halls on a building in the distance—Piper's destination. He'd just walk to the end of the alley, take a quick look around to make sure everything was okay, and then he'd go back and get his truck.

He reached the Dumpster. A sucker punch hit his jaw without warning. Then the man he'd been following leaped out from behind the trash, hands cocked to fight.

Benjamin stumbled and for an unsettling moment thought he was about to fall backward. But then he braced his feet and his grip held sure.

"Hey, man." Benjamin held his hands up and started into the man's ugly, scarred face. "I don't know what your problem is, but I don't want to fight."

Not because he didn't think he'd win. But because he really didn't like hurting people. Even sneering and snarling brutes who looked ready to pound him into the pavement.

"Nice try, but I ain't playing." The blond man pushed his sleeves up over his elbows, exposing muscular, tattoo-covered arms.

Including the tattoo of a brown bear and the word *Kodiak.*

Benjamin raised his fists to fight. He wasn't playing either. Not anymore.

A knife flashed in Kodiak's hand. Benjamin swung his bag out in front of him, catching the blow in the canvas. The bag ripped. Clothes and papers spilled out onto the ground.

Kodiak lunged at Benjamin.

Benjamin leaped sideways, but the knife tip came within an inch of piercing his stomach. His attacker stabbed again. This time Benjamin knocked the knife from Kodiak's hand and shoved him into the wall.

His forearm pressed into the man's neck, pinning him firmly. "What do you want? Why are you following Piper?"

"Hey, dude!" A voice floated down from the end of the alleyway. "I think that guy's beating up that other guy!"

Benjamin's head turned. Two teenagers stood at the end of the alley, their forms almost indistinguishable in puffy jackets and floppy tuques. Both clutched cell phones.

"Call the police," Benjamin shouted. "Now."

"Yeah!" Kodiak shouted. "He's got a knife. He's threatening to murder me. You got that? You tell the police. I was minding my own business and he attacked me."

Benjamin gritted his teeth and fought the urge to knock the lying thug's head against the wall. Neither boy was dialing. If anything, it looked as if they were either recording video or taking pictures. He winced to think of how this all must look from their perspective. They wouldn't see the man who cared for Piper battling the man who'd terrorized her. All they'd see were two large men, equally matched in size and strength, fighting in an alley—with one of them pinning the other up against the wall.

He could almost see the cover of the newspaper tabloid now: Notorious Snowmobile Accident Survivor Benji Duff Arrested in Niagara Region for Violent Street Fight. Pictures on Page Three.

Hardly the headline he wanted Meg waking up to on her wedding day.

Benjamin loosened his grip on his throat. "Look, I

don't want to hurt you. But I'm not going to let you get away with stalking and threatening Piper."

"I surrender. Okay?" Kodiak's hands inched up the wall. His fists were clenched. "Let's go to the police station together and let them sort it out. I'll tell them you followed me into this alley and I was only acting in self-defense."

They'd see how well that held up once Piper identified him as the man who tried to strangle her outside the barn.

"Okay." If Kodiak was willing to take this to the police station, even under duress, Benjamin didn't need to stand there insisting they fistfight. He stepped back, his foot nearly landing on the remains of his sliced hockey bag now lying on the grease-soaked ground. "We're going to walk nice and slow to the police station, and let them sort it out, all right?"

"Sure thing." Kodiak smirked. His fingers uncurled and the bright blue flame of a cigarette lighter flickered to life in his palm.

Benjamin lunged for the man's hand but it was too late.

Kodiak tossed the lighter down into the remains of Benjamin's oil-soaked belongings.

His bag caught fire.

EIGHT

Benjamin threw himself onto his belongings, pounding out the flames with his gloved hands before they could spread.

"Tell Piper I'll be seeing her." Kodiak spat a curse and sprinted back down the alley, knocking the two teenage gawkers aside like bowling pins.

Benjamin leaped to his feet and ran down the end of the alley, but Kodiak was already gone. So was the teenaged audience. Guess they'd seen no point in sticking around once the show was over. A large, rusty truck peeled out of the bar parking lot so quickly it fishtailed. A growl of frustration rumbled in the back of Benjamin's throat. At least Kodiak seemed to have gone in the opposite way from Piper this time.

Benjamin walked back down the alley, sat back on his heels in the slush and shoveled his belongings back into his bag as quickly as he could. A couple of his shirts were now nothing but rags and ashes. His favorite sweatshirt had a burn hole in it the size of his fist. But, thankfully his passport, traveling money and airline ticket had been spared.

He could buy a new bag on his way back to the island. He could grab a few new T-shirts and a sweat-shirt anywhere. But replacing the passport would have taken days. Maybe even weeks. His flight was not only nonrefundable, but he'd saved a bundle on airfare by flying on December 25. He'd have missed the start of the charity sailing race. Not to mention, every penny he'd made from selling his business was wrapped up in his boat or already converted into the starter money he was counting on to start his new charter-boat business.

Well, maybe it was a good thing he was leaving the country. That way God would find someone better to help protect Piper.

An ugly gash now ran along the length of his bag. He pulled a roll of duct tape from his bag, yanked off a strip and taped it shut.

His cell phone started ringing. It was Meg.

"Hello?"

"Hey, bro!" Her voice was so cheerful and hopeful he almost groaned. "Got your message about picking up the truck. How does it look?"

He glanced back at the brick wall behind him.

"I've reached the garage, but I haven't picked up the truck yet. Hang on." He yanked off two more strips of duct tape and made sure the hole was well patched. Then he grabbed the handles and stood up again. Slush and oil froze to his soaked jeans. "It's going to be a few more minutes before I can leave town. But I'll send you my GPS coordinates and route as soon as I hit the road."

There was a long pause. Then Meg said, "What happened?"

He trudged back down the alley toward the mechanic. "Don't worry about it. Please, I'll be on my way soon."

"Benji. Don't do this."

He sighed and leaned against the wall. "I saw the man who attacked Piper following her down an alley." He explained what happened. "I eased up because I'm a fool, and he got away."

Meg sighed. "You eased up on him because you're a good guy."

Yeah, but that still left Piper in serious danger.

And he didn't feel like much more than a waste of space right this second.

"Are you hurt?" she asked. "How's Piper?"

"Piper wasn't here. She doesn't know what happened. I'm fine. But my bag's seen better days." He glanced at the clock on his phone. It was almost twelve. "Obviously I have to talk to the police before I leave. The one piece of good news is that I saw his face, so I can give the cops a pretty solid description and hopefully they can catch the guy."

Although the fact the Kodiak was daring enough to attack him in broad daylight wasn't too comforting.

Another pause on the other end of the phone. "Are you going to go talk to Piper?"

"And tell her what, Meg? That I had the guy who attacked her in the palm of my hands and I let him go?"

"You need to tell her."

"I know." He ran his hand over the back of his neck, barely managing to stop himself when he remembered the muck he'd been kneeling in just moments before. "And yes, I know it's better to tell her in person than just call her. But I left things a bit…off with Piper when I said goodbye. I think I said something that hurt her feelings, and she kind of took off before I could really apologize properly. It's probably nothing. It just felt like a stormy goodbye."

And the news that he'd now let Kodiak escape wasn't going to help.

"What did you say to her?"

"I told her I wanted her to be happy, but it came out like I was insulting her decision to take care of her uncle and aunt." He blew out a hard breath and kept walking toward the police station. Picking up his truck would have to wait. "She's just so unhappy, Meg. Reminds me of how you used to be before Jack. She processes it very differently from you and tries to hide it. I don't think she'd admit it, even to herself."

"Well, there have been a couple of break-ins. Last night she was attacked."

"I know. But it's more than that. Last summer she was so happy, like there was all this light inside her. Now it's like she's killing herself to make other people happy. I was only trying to encourage her not to give up on her dreams, but somehow I messed the whole thing up."

Probably because she thought he wasn't listening and was just telling her she was wrong.

"So, go fix it."

He nearly laughed. Meg's advice sounded exactly like the kind of thing he'd said more times than he could count. *So, you messed up? Go fix it.*

Turned out the words felt a whole lot different on the receiving end.

Especially when he still had to file a police report, pick up his truck, talk things out with Piper and make it to his sister's wedding rehearsal. "I can't fix things with Piper now. The rehearsal's tonight and I'm seven hours away."

"Sure you can." Despite the rush and stress the bride must be feeling, he could still hear a smile in his sister's voice. "I'll move the rehearsal to nine or ten if we need to. Not like I'm going to be able to sleep tonight, anyway. Everything today got pushed back, anyway. Jack's best man, Luke, was delayed getting here from Muskoka because of the bad weather. So, that gives you a little more time. Not much. But enough that after you file a police report you can go find Piper, fill her in on what happened with Kodiak, say you're sorry for the misunderstanding earlier and try your hand at a better goodbye."

"I'm not sure I know how."

"You'll think of something." Warmth filled his sister's voice. "I have faith in you. Just make sure you make it back to the island tonight. There's still something very important I need to talk with you about at the wedding rehearsal."

His footsteps reached the police station. He glanced back at the clock. As long as he was on the road by two o'clock, he'd be okay. That gave him just two more hours. He set the alarm on his phone for a quarter to two, just to give him a small window to grab coffee before getting on the road. "Okay. Thanks. I'll be there, I promise. Love you."

"You, too. Now go file your report and say whatever needs saying to Piper."

Whatever needed saying. Okay, but what was that? He still meant every word he'd said to Piper, despite the fact he'd somehow mangled them and said them in a way that upset her.

Now he was skating in overtime, had just let the opponent deke a shot past him and still didn't know how to make things right.

The retirement home was a large beige rectangular building with featureless square windows. Ornate letters on the door read Silver Halls but didn't do anything to change the fact that the structure looked like a cardboard box. He walked through the front door and crossed through a lobby with blue-tiled floors. Bits of silver tinsel draped limply over fake plants. A few velvet bows were clipped haphazardly onto the plastic leaves.

A young woman who didn't look much more than eighteen sat at the front desk. She didn't move, and barely even glanced his way when he walked in.

He raised a hand. "Hi. I'm looking for my friend Piper Lawrence. She's here visiting her uncle and aunt?"

The receptionist shrugged toward the doorway on the other side of the room and then looked back down at her cell phone, which he took as an invitation to walk in. A pair of open, shuttered doors led to a long, multipurpose room. The carpet was industrial green; the air smelled like disinfectant mixed with peppermint air freshener. He glanced out the nearest window and saw the wall of the apartment building next door.

While The Downs wasn't exactly his cup of tea, either, he knew which place he'd choose to live out his last days.

Then he saw the couple. They were sitting together with their backs to him, on a settee on the far side of the room. The man was tall and bald, with a soft green holiday sweater and one arm around the woman curled up next to him. Her long salt-and-pepper hair fell lush against his shoulder. A plain gold wedding band shone on his hand. She leaned toward him and said something Benjamin couldn't hear. He turned toward her, with a look both so tender and caring, it suddenly reminded Benjamin of the couple, half their age, whose wedding he was going to witness tomorrow. The woman's eyes twinkled. Her husband brushed a quick kiss across her lips.

Benjamin turned away, feeling like an intruder on their private moment. An unexpected ache clenched his heart. The couple must be older than his own parents, by a few years, at least. Yet, he'd never seen his father look at his mother with that kind of tender, loving respect. Nor his mother look at his father with such trust. True, they'd kept their marriage going all these years, which was something, and he'd barely seen them since they'd retired and moved to Florida.

He thought of Meg and Jack. There was something so raw, vibrant and real about the love he'd watched grow between them in the past year and a half. He hoped they'd never lose that.

"Benjamin!" Piper's voice broke into his thoughts. "Come meet my aunt and uncle." A smile of surprise lit her eyes as she hurried across the floor.

"Hi!" Her hand brushed along his side in a gesture that was half like a hug and half like pulling him toward her.

"Hi." His cheeks felt warm.

"What are you doing here?" Her fingers curled lightly into the fabric of his coat. "What happened with your truck? Is everything okay?"

How did he put this?

"Well, the good news is that the police think they might have a lead on Kodiak. I'll fill you in on the rest after I meet your uncle and aunt. I've got almost an hour and a half before I need to leave."

The happiness glittered in her eyes. "Well, whatever it is, I'm glad you came to talk it out with me in person. I'll do my best to keep this brief." Her hand brushed over his. She steered him toward the couple on the settee. "Uncle Des, Aunt Cass, I'd like you to meet my friend Benjamin Duff. Benjamin, meet my uncle and aunt, Desmond and Cassandra Lawrence."

It seemed fitting that Piper had their last name, as opposed to the surname of the father who had abandoned her.

Benjamin smiled. "It's very nice to meet you."

Des didn't stand. But his grip was firm and his eyes were clear. "Nice to meet you."

It was then that Benjamin noticed the walker tucked against the wall. Just how bad were Piper's aunt's health problems?

"Please, sit." Cass took his outstretched hand in both of hers. Her hands were delicate, soft. Like her husband, Piper's aunt still had a strong British accent. "Piper and I were just talking decorations."

Benjamin found himself pulled down onto the settee. Cass slid a large photo album onto his lap. Piper held up her fingers and mouthed, *Ten minutes. Okay?*

He nodded. He looked down at the pages. They were photos of a small English village. A beautiful ridge of mountains lay on one side, the rocky shore and gray expanse of the waters of the English Channel lay on the other. Beautiful shops and town houses wound through the narrow streets, wreathed in pine branches, large wide bows and sprigs of real holly. There was just the faintest dusting of snow on the ground.

"Have you ever been to the south of England, son?" Des asked.

Benjamin nodded. "Yes, sir. I've taken part in a couple of sailing tournaments out of a wonderful extreme sports resort and marina run by a friend just outside Brighton and traveled the coast in both directions. It's a wonderful place."

"It is." Cass's eyes shone as he turned the page.

Benjamin sat for a moment and just listened, turning the pages as instructed, and listening as the older woman pointed out the buildings and streets of her childhood. Piper sat on the footstool beside him and leaned back against his legs. "My aunt and I often look to her Christmases back home as inspiration for Christmas Eve at The Downs."

"Oh, we had beautiful Christmases there." Cass smiled softly. "We didn't get the piles of snow you do here. Just enough to make the world feel special. Our church would do a special dinner for the community. We used to roast chestnuts."

Her eyes misted softly.

Her husband slid his hands over hers. "Cassy didn't know what she was getting into when she married a man who was headed to Canada forty-two years ago."

She smiled softly, and poked her husband in the ribs. "Of course I did."

Des looked down at his wife. "Yes, but the plan always was that we were going to go back."

Her eyes met his. "Plans change."

Benjamin nodded slowly. Yeah, sometimes they did. Remodeling the beloved bed-and-breakfast to make it accessible might be hard, but it still had to be a lot easier than packing up their lives and moving back overseas at their age and stage of life.

"Have you managed to chop down a tree yet?" Cass asked Piper.

"No, not yet. Time sort of got away from me today."

Benjamin glanced at the clock. "How about I go help you chop down a tree? I've still got some time before I need to leave. My sister's delayed the wedding rehearsal until nine tonight."

Besides, maybe both conversations they needed to have would be easier if he knew he'd managed to do something productive.

She nodded. "Thank you."

They didn't talk much on the drive to the Christmas-tree farm. Benjamin focused his attention on steering down the unpaved back roads through the woods, while Piper gave directions. It was only when the truck came to a stop and he turned off the engine that she turned to him on the seat.

She looked down. "I'm really glad you got a chance to meet Uncle Des and Aunt Cass. They are the most solid people and I've always been able to count on them. I owe them my life."

Then her eyes met his, and for a moment there was something in their depths that reminded him of the rush he got the first time he set eyes on a new path of wilderness. Boundless. Fathomless. Filled with await-ing adventures.

His rational mind kicked him to say what he needed to say. But something deep in his chest rebelled. He needed to tell her he'd had a run-in with Kodiak and let him escape. But first, maybe they should just relax and enjoy this moment. It might be their last chance to ever be alone.

They got out of the truck and walked through the woods without talking, enjoying the easy, comfortable silence they'd fallen into back on the island. Her dark hair was tucked behind her ear, under her bright blue tuque, falling in dark waves around her shoulders in between the folds of her scarf. Snowflakes fell from the sky and swirled around them on the breeze. A glimmer of a smile curled at the corner of her lips.

This was the Piper he remembered from the summer. This was the Piper who'd made him excited to get up out of bed every morning. This was the Piper he'd—

The train of thought caught him up short and made a freezing cold breath catch in his lungs.

He'd what exactly? Been attracted to? Been drawn to?

Had felt himself falling for until his sister reminded him how foolhardy that would be?

"This'll do. Don't you think?" Piper stopped in front of a fir tree, at least fifteen feet tall, he'd guess, with thick, lush branches.

"It's a beauty all right." He let her pull the ax from his hands. "How were you ever going to cart a tree like this back to the barn by yourself?"

"Oh, I'd have figured something out." She gripped the ax with both hands and swung. The loud, satisfying sound of the ax hitting the wood echoed through the forest. Her grin grew wider.

His eyes rose to the heavens.

Lord, my flight's in two days' time. How can I get on that plane without knowing that Piper is perfectly, totally and utterly safe?

The sound of Piper's ax swings filled the air around them. He closed his eyes as his prayer deepened.

But I want so much more for her than just safety. I want her to be happy. I want her to have everything she's hoping for, everything she's dreamed of, every adventure she's capable of having.

His heart ached knowing he'd never be the one to give all that to her.

He opened his eyes again, and stared at the ice-covered tree branches above him.

"Timber." Piper stood back as the tree fell into the snow. "I've always loved *this* part. I might not be as big a fan as Aunt Cass of decorating or planning meals, but I could be out here chopping trees for hours."

"Well, it suits you."

Piper swirled the ax around in slow motion. "You think I should give up the bed-and-breakfast business to become a lumberjack?"

"No, I think you should come sail the world with my friends and me."

NINE

Piper's jaw dropped. The ax slipped from her hands and sank into the snow at her feet.

"There are several boats on this sailing trip, not just mine." Benjamin said it so casually, as if he was just inviting her to join him and some buddies for pizza. "One's an all-women crew and I'm sure they'd have an extra bunk if you wanted to join us for even part of the journey. A few months or a few weeks. Whatever. It wouldn't have to be a big thing."

Right, because spending thousands of dollars to fly overseas and go sailing for a while wasn't a "big thing" at all. Not to mention her responsibilities here.

He ran his hand over the back of his neck. "Bring a friend if you'd like and we'll find a space for them, too. I don't even know half of the people I'll be sailing with. It's no biggie."

So now he'd pointed out twice how little the invitation meant to him.

She held his gaze for a long moment. Then she bent down and picked up the ax. "Thank you for the suggestion, but that's not really something I'd be able to do."

Even if she did have the time and the money—which

she didn't—how could she possibly consider flying halfway around the world to spend time with someone who'd take something like that so casually? It had been hard enough to forgive her father for bailing on them when she was little and forgive her mom for chasing after a whole string of temporary relationships with men just as unwilling to stay. When Benjamin had walked into the retirement home like that for a split second she'd almost let herself believe that it meant something.

He reached into his pocket, pulled out a thick ball of twine and carefully helped her bind the branches. "I mean, obviously, you're not going anywhere until those renovations are saved up for and sorted, and your uncle and aunt are able to move back in. But the initial trip will be about a year, and there will hopefully be more group trips after that."

"Thanks. But I won't be going anywhere, even after the renovations are done."

"Oh. All right, then." His shoulders dropped as if she'd just let the air out of his chest.

They dragged the tree back to the truck in silence and drove back to The Downs.

Piper's eyes stayed locked on the window.

"I hope I didn't say the wrong thing or offend you when I suggested you take a holiday from The Downs," Benjamin said when he'd pulled his truck past the bed-and-breakfast driveway, down the hill and up to the barn. "Your uncle and aunt are obviously amazing people. I know how much they mean to you and I really respect your dedication to running The Downs."

She pressed her lips together but didn't trust herself to speak. Was she being oversensitive? After all, it was hardly Benjamin's fault that he didn't realize how serious her aunt's health problems were. She hadn't told him. But she didn't know where to start.

The whole thing felt so huge and unwieldy in her head. It was the kind of conversation that took time. Time they didn't have.

She turned away from him and looked out her window. All around the property the trees were bent low and some had split from the weight of the ice. A fleeting shadow on the barn roof caught her eye. *Please, not raccoons on top of everything else.* There had to be at least six feet of snow on the barn roof and by the looks of things the branches of a huge tree were practically smacking the roof in the wind. She should really cut some before one cracked off and fell through the roof.

Benjamin's eyes glanced at the cell phone mounted in the cradle on the dash. Her eyes followed. Twenty minutes, then he had to go.

Piper undid her seat belt and opened her door. Then she stopped, sat back against her seat and wrapped her arms around herself.

Lord, I need something solid right now. Everything seems to be crumbling around me right now. And my aunt, the strongest, most solid woman I know, is withering away in front of me.

"Hey," he said softly. "Everything okay?"

"Aunt Cass couldn't brush her hair this morning. My uncle brushed it for her, even though it probably hurt him a ton because of his arthritis. Not that he'd ever complain." She ran both hands over her eyes. "Doctors don't know what's wrong with her yet. Her limbs are just kind of numb sometimes and don't work like they should. We're still in that phase where it's all tests and waiting."

"I'm sorry." His voice was so soft it was barely more than a whisper.

"It's okay. That's the way life is sometimes, I guess. But you asked me what's wrong with her. I don't know what to say, because we really don't know. I mean, when you hear words like amyotrophic lateral sclerosis or multiple sclerosis they sound like they should be kind of the same thing, but in reality they're different and would mean totally different things for her life expectancy or the kind of help she's going to need in the future. And those are just two of the many things doctors haven't actually ruled out yet."

His hand was lying right there on the front seat between them. She reached for it. He wrapped her hand in his and held it tightly.

"Maybe she only has a couple of years left to live, in which case I'm not about to head off on some fantastic trip overseas. I'm going to be here for whatever time she has left. Or maybe she's going to outlive Uncle Des by a decade or more, in which case she's going to need someone to live with and make her tea, brush her hair, fix her meals, run The Downs…"

Tears choked the words from her throat. Did he have any idea how helpless this whole situation made her feel? Yeah, more than anyone, Benjamin probably would.

"And you're going to be there for them." Benjamin slid across the seat and wrapped his arms around her. "No matter what they need. You're going to be there."

She let her head fall against his shoulder. "Yes. I really will."

Because they took me in where my father abandoned us. Because they raised me when my mom kept wanting to run off chasing whichever man turned her head. Because I love them. Because they're my family.

A tear slipped down her cheek. He held her tighter.

"I want to apologize." His lips brushed the top of her head. "I'm really sorry if I ever made it sound like I don't respect the sacrifices you're making or how hard you're working. I think you're doing an amazing job. I respect you so much—you have no idea."

For a long moment she didn't say anything. She just let her body lay in his strength and watched the minutes count down until Benjamin had to leave. Tears filled her eyes and fought to escape her eyelashes. She didn't pull away. He didn't her let go.

"Remember that feeling of helplessness?" she asked, "Like everything's falling apart and you can't do anything to stop it?"

"I really do. In fact, I feel pretty helpless right now." Benjamin's voice dropped. She turned around until they were facing each other. His left hand spread across the small of her back, as his right slid up her cheek. His fingers brushed a tear from the corner of her eye. "I haven't actually felt this helpless since I was lying flat on my back in a hospital bed with all four limbs in a cast. Only that time was almost easier because the pain was mine to fight. This time it's not. The pain is yours and I can't figure out how fix it, even though I'd do anything in my power to make things right for you."

"I know." She leaned her forehead against his. "And you can't. But thank you for wanting to."

She closed her eyes. She could feel him there, breathing the same inch of frosty air, her tears brushing the soft scruff of his jaw.

Then slowly, as naturally as breathing, his lips found

hers. They'd barely met when a loud, incessant ringing filled the cab.

"Your phone!" She pulled back from the kiss.

Benjamin leaped back so quickly his head bumped against the roof. "That's not my phone. Mine's not ringing."

"Well, I don't have a cell phone. Mine was destroyed yesterday."

The ringing grew louder and seemed to be coming from the backseat. Benjamin reached around behind him and yanked his bag into his lap. Her jaw dropped. What had he done to his bag? It was filthy and patched with duct tape.

He ripped back the zipper, rummaged around inside and pulled out a phone. "This isn't mine. I must have accidentally picked it up from the alley."

"The alley? What alley?"

He glanced at the screen. His face paled.

"Benjamin, what's going on?"

He held up the phone toward her.

And she saw who the incoming call was from.

Alpha.

TEN

Benjamin stared in disbelief at the ringing phone in his hands. Kodiak must have dropped his phone in the alleyway during the fight and, somehow in all the confusion, Benjamin had scooped it into his bag with his things.

And now Alpha was calling it.

Piper was staring at him now. Her hands rose to her lips. "Why is Alpha calling you?"

"He's not calling me. This is obviously Kodiak's phone and I picked it up by mistake when we fought in the alley." But now what? The only question that really mattered now was whether or not he should risk answering it. His gut was dying to, but if Alpha realized someone else had Kodiak's phone, it could rob the police of a valuable lead. *Lord, I don't know what to do—*

"I don't understand what's happening here." Piper's voice rose. "What fight in what alley?"

The phone stopped ringing.

Benjamin sighed. Probably just as well he hadn't answered it.

He looked at her. "After you dropped me off at the garage, I saw a man walk into the alley after you. It was same man we saw smoking outside the bar and I thought he might be following you, so I followed him. He jumped me and we fought. Turned out to be Kodiak."

Her eyes grew wide.

He glanced down at the phone. The screen read: *Missed Call.*

"And then?" Piper was still looking at him. Not at the phone in his hand. At him.

"Then he got away, I went to report it to the police and then came to find you and tell you about it." *Only I didn't tell you. I held off because you seemed to be happy and that made me happy, and I didn't want to ruin the moment.* In fact, he basically tried to leave it to the last possible second. And then, he'd gotten swept up in the feeling of her in his arms, and he'd kissed her. He couldn't begin to guess what she might think of him now. He didn't even know what to think of himself. "But that's the reason my sister agreed to delay the rehearsal."

"Oh." Piper sat back on the passenger seat. "So, that's why you hadn't left town yet."

"Well, yeah. Why else did you think I'd still be sticking around here?"

Piper's eyes dropped to her knees.

Oh. Guilt stabbed Benjamin's heart. She'd thought he'd come back for her.

The phone started to buzz as texts appeared rapid-fire on the screen.

When I call your phone I expect you to answer!

Did you find Charlotte?

Answer me!

Did you find her?

She told me she was going to the Downs for Christmas!

The messages stopped. Piper leaned in and read over Benjamin's shoulder.

"He still thinks Kodiak has his phone," she said. "And apparently Charlotte told him she was coming here. Although there's no reason why she couldn't have been lying about that."

He nodded. "Looks that way." Now he was grateful he hadn't answered the phone call. These texts might actually lead to something useful.

The messages faded from the screen. He pressed the unlock button to read them again, but the phone demanded a password. He set it down on the dashboard. "I'm going to drop it off to the police on my way out of town. I was already able to give them a good description of Kodiak without a mask on. Might take them a few days, but hopefully between the phone and that description they'll have enough to be able to catch the guy."

She shook her head, then looked straight ahead to the snow falling thick and fresh on the windshield. "You should have told me. Right away. Kodiak tried to kill me. You had no right to hide something like that from me."

"You were already dealing with a lot." Heat rose to the back of his neck. "I was trying to protect you."

She spun back. Her eyes flashed at him. "I never asked you to protect me."

The phone began to buzz again, rattling across the dashboard toward Piper. She caught it and held the screen up where they could both see it.

Hello? Hello?

Where are you?

She said something about a Christmas thing. Did you check all the Christmas things?

Did you check the brick? I think I heard her say something about bricks to that guy.

You know, that guy she's cheating on me with!

If you find and hurt the guy she's cheating on me with I'll pay you double.

Fifty thou for bringing me her. Fifty thou for killing him. Got it?

Got it?

You're starting to make me mad.

Get to the usual place now and wait for me.

I'm not texting you again! So you'd better get there. Now. Or you'll be sorry.

After the wild flurry of texts, Kodiak's phone fell silent again. A shiver ran down Benjamin's neck. Whoever this Alpha was he sounded both psychotic and dangerous.

And there was only one other young man he'd met

recently who had that bad impulse control. *Gavin.* "I don't like this."

Piper sucked in a deep breath as she wrapped her arms around her body. "Neither do I. It's all too fresh. It's like six years ago all over again. Exactly like six years ago. Like I'm twenty again and Charlotte is coming here for Christmas. I feel like I'm stuck in a time loop where history's repeating itself."

"Do you have any idea why she'd come here for Christmas this year? Or what he could possibly mean about Christmas things or bricks?"

She looked so lost that for a moment it took every impulse in his body not to reach out and hold her. "No. I wish I did. But I don't."

The cell phone began to chime. But this time it wasn't Kodiak's with a new text message. It was his phone alarm. He groaned.

"Piper, I'm sorry. I'm so very sorry. But I have to go. I promised my sister I'd hit the road by two... And I... I didn't expect to take this long."

"Okay. Let's get the tree off your truck and into the barn. Then you can drop me and Kodiak's phone off at the police station. I'll call Dominic to come pick me up from there."

Piper jumped out into the snow. It was falling thicker and faster now than the forecast had called for. The door slammed behind her. Seconds later she was hauling the tree off the back of the truck without even waiting for him. He slipped the phone into one of the oversize pockets of his winter jacket, along with his army knife and windup flashlight. Then he hopped out. "Here, let me help with that. You take the top, I'll take the bottom."

"Makes sense." She stopped. "But then I've got another favor to ask you, okay?"

"All right. Anything."

She stood there a moment, under a dark gray sky, her eyes on his face, and his eyes on hers, as if they were tied there by some invisible string.

"After we take the tree into the barn and you drop me off at the police station, you're just going to go. Okay? No speeches. No big affectionate gestures. Don't even say goodbye. Give me a quick hug, like a friend would do, and go. Head to your sister's wedding. Head off to the other side of the world and enjoy your life." Piper crossed her arms. "Stop worrying about me. Please. Don't worry, not about me, or The Downs, or my aunt's health, or whether I'll be taking smart precautions to protect myself from Alpha. I know you're a good guy. I know you want to help me and rescue me. But I'm fine. I promise you. This isn't some trap I'm stuck in. This is my life. I've chosen it and I'm going to manage it. I don't need saving."

He nodded slowly. "Got it."

He grabbed the other end of the tree and helped her carry it through the snow and up the stairs. They stepped inside the cold, dark barn and set down the tree. The power was still off so he pulled a windup flashlight from his pocket and shone the beam back and forth over the room. As he did, a cry slipped through Piper's lips.

The barn had been trashed. Tables were knocked over. Boxes of decorations were scattered across the floor. Stacks of chairs had been tossed. The cement in the fireplace looked as if someone had taken a couple of whacks at it with a sledgehammer. Even the hay under the wooden loft overhang had been torn into shreds and tossed.

"I don't understand!" Piper's hands rose in exasperation. "I don't know what I ever did to Charlotte that she decided to trash our Christmas decorations six years ago. I don't know why she'd ever come back here now! Let alone why she'd drag her abusive former boyfriend into this and some other guy he thinks she's cheating on him with." Her arms spun toward the wreckage. "Is this what Alpha meant by checking the 'Christmas things'? Did Charlotte do this? Did Kodiak or Blondie or someone else Alpha sent after her?"

Benjamin ached to go to her, to hold her, to make it right. Yet she'd demanded a promise from him and he'd given it. But, how could he just leave Piper and not try to help her now?

The barn door slammed shut, plunging the air around them into a deep murky gloom. Piper strode over to the door and pulled. The door didn't move. She tossed down her gloves, gripped it with her bare hands and pulled harder.

"Everything okay?"

She shook her head hard, tossing her hair. "No. I can't even budge it."

A loud crack boomed through the air above them. Then came a creak from above, as if something was trying to split the roof like a giant nutcracker.

Benjamin grabbed Piper's arm and pulled her into the soft hay pile under the loft.

"Get down!"

An avalanche of wood and snow caved in on top of them.

ELEVEN

Piper was so cold. That was the only thought that went through her head as she opened her eyes to survey her surroundings. But she saw only dark blurs. Her glasses were gone. She tried to move, but her frozen legs would not budge. She was wedged in, snow pressing in to the right and left of her legs. Able to move her arms, she felt around in the darkness. Snow formed a wall all around her, and thick wooden planks crossed just inches above her head.

Fighting panic, her mind scrambled to focus. Memories assailed her, one at a time.

There had been a loud cracking noise. Benjamin threw her into the hay. The roof caved in on top of them.

Then the barn had collapsed, burying them alive.

She closed her eyes again as tears ran down her cheeks. *Lord, I'm scared. I'm trapped. I don't know what to do.*

There was a groan to her right.

"Benjamin?" She turned toward the sound. Her bare fingers dug in the densely packed snow. "I'm here. Can you hear me? I'm coming to you."

The groaning grew louder. She dug furiously, until

her fist punched through the snow wall and into another larger air pocket. She scrabbled away at the hole until she could slide her body through. She turned onto her hands and knees and crawled forward in the darkness. Her hand brushed against something soft. Her fingers trailed up the lines of Benjamin's coat, to his shoulder, then finally onto his soft beard. Then she felt a hand brush hers.

"Piper." Benjamin's fingers looped through hers. "Are you okay?"

"My body seems to still be in one piece and everything's moving all right." She tried to get up, but the ceiling of the pocket was barely a foot above her head. "How about you?"

"Yeah. I'm okay. Just sore. I think I bumped my head, but I've felt worse."

She curled into the snow beside him. "I'm sorry you're going to be late for your sister's wedding rehearsal."

A chuckle slipped through his lips. "Yup. Well, one problem at a time. Right now I'm going to worry about getting us out of here. I'm guessing there are several feet of snow on top of us now, along with a bunch of broken boards and pieces of the barn roof. Hang on, I think I'm sitting on the flashlight." He dropped her hand. She heard a whirring sound, then a bright light flashed across her eyes, replacing the gray spots with yellow spots. She blinked and saw nothing but splotches.

"Hey," his voice dropped. One hand reached up the side of her face, brushing along her skin. "You don't have your glasses."

She shook her head. "They're gone. Somewhere. I can't see a thing. Just shadows of light and darkness."

"Don't worry about that. We'll figure something out." He wrapped one arm around her and squeezed her tight. The warm, rough wool of his coat pressed against her cheek. He kissed the top of her head. "Just give me a moment to look around and think, then we'll come up with a plan. Don't worry."

How could she not worry? She was terrified. As silly as it would probably sound if she admitted it, not being able to see was scaring her more than being crushed by snow and a falling roof.

She clenched her jaw and told herself to be strong. But still she could feel the tears there, pooling in her eyes. She blinked hard and for a fraction of a moment thought she'd regained control. Then she felt a treacherous tear slip down her cheek.

No. I won't cry again. Not in front of Benjamin.

He shifted sideways, as if changing his angle, and pushed her back into the snow. "Oh, I'm sorry. I should have warned you before moving."

"Just focus on finding us a way out."

"I remember from spelunking over the summer how being in tight spaces kind of bothers you."

Bothered her? She could feel a sob building in the back of her throat and hoped he hadn't been able to hear it in her voice. She felt far more than bothered. She felt helpless. What's more she hated that this was probably how Benjamin would remember her now: blind, trapped, scared—and kissing him back in the truck when she should have been strong enough to push him away.

"Charlotte locked me in the kindling box." The words were out before she could rethink them. "At least, I think it was her."

"What?" Benjamin's body froze. "That's terrible."

"Yeah, it really was." She couldn't make out the features of his face without her glasses. But she could feel him there, his breath on her face and his chest rising and falling softly. "I'd been in this barn, with Uncle Des, Aunt Cass and everyone celebrating Christmas Eve. I should've stayed. But I saw Charlotte slip out and tried to follow her. I didn't even make it back to the house before someone—and I've always been pretty sure it was Charlotte—hit me on the head, shoved me into the box and locked me in. It was half an hour probably before Dominic found me. I'm just thankful he noticed I'd left and went looking for me. I don't know if I was more scared or angry. But ever since then I panic in closed spaces."

Benjamin pulled her tighter. "I was terrified in traction after the snowmobile accident because doctors didn't know at first how I'd recover. But I was livid with myself, too. I was so angry with myself for putting the people I loved through that. I promised myself that I would never put myself in a situation where I could break someone's heart like that, and that once I was able to run I'd never let myself get trapped ever again." His hand brushed her back. "But as much as I hate being trapped right now, at least I'm trapped with you."

She let out a long breath. Funny, as much as she liked Benjamin, right now, if she had a choice of whom to be trapped with it wouldn't be someone who'd be sprinting to their truck the moment they broke through the snow.

"How big is the hole we're trapped in?" she asked.

The flashlight started to whirr again. "I'd say four feet high, eight feet long and about six feet wide."

That meant they probably had thirty minutes of air,

maybe more, depending on whether they could find a ventilation hole. It was now a question of whether accidentally causing a cave-in by rushing to dig a way out was more or less dangerous than taking their time and maybe running out of air.

She wondered how it all happened. "Did a tree fall through the roof?"

"Maybe," he said. "We're under a pile of broken wood right now. There's a solid wall of wood to our right, which has kind of splintered in. On the other side there's a lot of snow, with a hole."

"Yeah, that's where I was buried."

He shifted away from her. "I've got to be careful, otherwise this whole thing could come toppling in on us."

Light and dark shapes and shadows swam in front of her eyes. She had backup glasses back at The Downs, but for now she might as well be blind. Frustration screamed inside her, but she swallowed it back. She might not be able to help Benjamin, but at the very least, she didn't need to make things harder for him.

"Hang on," he said. "There's what looks like a branch just above us to the left. I'm going to try to move it an inch or two and see what happens. We might be able to create a small ventilation pocket. Also, it might give us an idea of just how deep this mess is. We might even be able to just dig a hole and climb straight up. Just stay back and out of the way."

She couldn't see well enough to even know what constituted "out of the way." Still, she curled into a ball and slid back until she felt snow against her back.

"Okay…it's moving. Which is good. I'm just going to try to— Oh, Lord, please help us!"

His sudden, shouted prayer was swallowed by the

rush of falling wood and snow. Piper tucked her head into her knees and cradled her arms above it. Benjamin's arms flew around her, sheltering her body with his. Silent prayers flew from her lips, mingled with the pleas for safety coming from Benjamin's.

Finally the rushing of snow stopped. When silence fell, Benjamin sat back and loosened his arms. "I'm really, really sorry about that. You okay?"

"It's not your fault. You had no way of knowing." But now she was buried in snow up to her waist. "I'm fine. Cold, though. Feels like my legs are frozen."

"The bad news is we're now in a lot smaller space," he said. "The good news is we still have the flashlight. I'd suggest we climb straight up, but there are broken boards and nails everywhere. Not to mention there's probably a big heavy tree somewhere over our heads." He sighed loudly. "It's like being trapped inside one of those wooden puzzles where if you pull the wrong thing it all crashes down, with us inside, and I pulled the wrong piece. In the meantime, let's focus on keeping warm while I figure this out."

He unzipped his coat and pulled her into his chest. Warmth radiated from his body into hers. The flashlight started up again. She waited, curled against his chest, tucked in the strength of his arms and battling the urge to cry. Her mind yelled at her to be stronger than this. She should be figuring a way out of this, not lying buried in the snow, in the arms of the man she'd fought so hard not to let herself fall in love with.

But what good am I right now if all I can see are blobs of light and shadows?

She took a deep breath. "Turn off the flashlight,

please. I want to give my eyes a moment to adjust to the darkness and look for something."

The whirring stopped. "But I thought you couldn't see anything."

"Yeah," she said. "But when you've spent your entire life figuring out one set of blobs from another every time you're in the dark and need to find your glasses, you also get surprisingly good at telling shadows apart."

The light slowly dimmed to black. Slowly she turned her head, scanning every inch of the infuriatingly indistinct shades of light and dark gray that swam past her eyes.

Lord, help me now. If there's something I'm supposed to see, help me see it.

"There!" She pointed. "There's a light source over there. It's like the change you see behind your eyelids when you turn toward a light with your eyes closed. We need to dig in that direction."

There was a long pause. Then he said, "Okay. We dig in that direction. We tried it my way earlier. Now we'll try yours."

He started to dig. She closed her eyes and prayed not to feel another rush of snow caving in on top of them.

"Okay," he said after a long moment. 'I've got a bit of a tunnel dug now. I'm going to crawl in and keep digging. Just feel for my foot, and you can follow me out."

She didn't miss the irony. She'd distanced herself from Benjamin after the summer because she didn't want to foolishly chase after a man who'd just end up breaking her heart. Now she was literally following him blindly.

"Quiet." His hand brushed her arm to still her. "Listen."

She focused her ears on the silence. Then she heard it—barking and then Dominic shouting her name.

"Hey! Hey! We're in here!" they shouted back.

As Benjamin dug faster, hope leaped in her chest. After a few moments light burst through her vision, then a large bundle of fur landed on her chest. *Thank You, God!*

"Hey, you okay?" Dominic's voice came from above her.

"Yeah," was all she could manage to say.

Benjamin stood up. "We were in the barn and the roof caved in. Piper, it looks like a pretty major tree fell."

"That's some dog you've got," Dominic said to her. "Practically dragged me out of the house and then wouldn't let me rest until I found you two."

She felt his hand on her arm ready to help her up. Instead, she stayed on her knees for a moment and wrapped her arms around Harry. The dog licked her face.

She was out. She was alive. She was safe.

Benjamin might even make it back to the island before the wedding rehearsal was over.

"Hey." Benjamin's voice floated over the air. "What happened to my truck?"

TWELVE

Benjamin looked down onto the living room from the second-story balcony as he dialed his sister's cell phone number. Below him, Piper was curled up on the sofa in front of the fire, blue backup glasses on her nose and a blue-and-white Maple Leafs hockey jersey draped over her frame. A police officer and Dominic flanked her on either side and the dog was curled in a ball at her feet. The grandfather clock read four thirty.

Meg answered on the first ring. "Benji?"

He turned his back on the scene below. There was no easy way to say this. "My truck's been stolen. I'm not going to make it to the rehearsal."

His sister sighed. "But are you okay?"

"Yeah." He slid all the way down until he was sitting on the floor. "But I had everything in that truck—my bag, my passport, my airline ticket, emergency credit card, traveling money. It's all gone. Literally all I have now is my driver's license and twenty bucks."

She gasped. "Oh, Benji, I'm so sorry."

"Yeah, sis. Me, too." He stared up at the wooden beams crossing above as wind howled outside. The predicted storm had arrived full force, bringing heavy snow once again. The town was still without power, but Dominic had brought over a portable generator and hooked it up to a few essential circuits, including a couple of standing lamps. "A friend of Piper's has offered to lend me his car, as long as somebody's able to drive it back down to him after the wedding."

"Of course, we have several guests heading back that way. But what about your flight?"

Benjamin blew out a long breath. "Doesn't look good. It's unlikely I'll be able to get a new passport issued in time, not with everything being shut down for Christmas. And the airline won't refund my flight. I'm just hoping that once I get home to the island and visit a government office there, they'll be able to do something. I'm about to hit the road now and I'll grab food on the way. I should be there around midnight."

"The bridge to the island is closing tonight until tomorrow morning," Meg said gently. "It's iced up and they're saying a whole lot of snow is going to keep falling overnight. Stay there, get some sleep and get here as soon as you can in the morning."

"But tomorrow's your wedding!"

"Yup. Ironic, I know. I'm a wedding planner who spent years panicking about the safety of her baby brother, and now circumstances are conspiring to keep you from making it to my wedding. The old Meg would be hanging from the ceiling by her fingernails." She chuckled. "Maybe God's showing me just how far I've come in the past year and a half, and just how ready I am to marry Jack tomorrow. Fortunately, all the other guests have now made it here safe and sound. We'll all pray that you make it here on time."

He closed his eyes and dropped his head into his

hands. "But what if something happens and I don't make it?"

"You will. I'll dance with you at the reception, open presents with you Christmas morning and have Christmas brunch with you and the family before you leave for Australia and we leave for our honeymoon."

"Okay." He closed his eyes. He was exhausted and couldn't help feeling he was letting his sister down on the most important day of her life. The fact she was being so awesome about it didn't make him feel any better.

The gentle murmur of Piper's voice floated up through the air behind him. Even though he couldn't make out her words the mere tone of her voice seemed to brush the back of his neck like gentle fingertips, calming him a bit. He was so frustrated right now he was ready to grab Piper's boxing gloves and start punching at the snow. Meg had tried to warn him about showing up in person to drop off the dog. But he hadn't listened. Now he was messing up his sister's wedding plans. And all he'd succeeded in doing with Piper was letting the man who'd attacked her escape, fumbling another goodbye and kissing her.

If he hadn't decided to drop Harry off in person, Piper might never have been at the barn so late that Kodiak was able to attack her like that. Yes, Benjamin had stepped in to protect her, twice. But if he hadn't been here, wouldn't God have provided someone else? A better guardian? Somebody smarter and wiser than he had been? His sister had been right. He never should have insisted on driving down and dropping the dog off himself. He'd selfishly given in to his own desire to take one last look at Piper. Hadn't he learned anything from hearing Piper's stories? Her life had been damaged enough by selfish people—her father, her mother, Charlotte and the evil, cruel brutes who were threatening her now. It didn't matter that his heart was in the right place. Piper needed stable people to stand by her. Not the kind of man who was going to give her a quick hug—let alone a reckless kiss—before dashing off to chase his own dreams.

Well, Lord, I'm just going to have to trust that You have Piper's back and will help surround her with the kind of people she needs.

"Don't worry." His sister's voice drifted down the line. "Everything's going to be okay."

He should be the one standing there, in person, telling her that. "There was something you wanted to talk to me about at the rehearsal—"

"Don't worry about that right now."

"You told me it was important."

"Yes, but not as important as you just getting here safe." She was using her "I'm trying to protect you" tone of voice. It bothered him just as much as it probably bothered Piper when he did it.

"Sis? Just tell me."

She sighed. "I was going to ask you to walk me down the aisle tomorrow."

He felt his breath leave him, as if someone had just sucker punched him in the gut. Certainly he'd known she wasn't going to ask their father to do it; he'd never been emotionally there for her. But Benjamin had never imagined... "I thought you'd decided to walk in alone."

"I wanted to tell you in person." Sounded as if there were tears in Meg's voice, too. "Jack and I are having all four of our parents come in together. Then he's com-

ing in with his best man, Luke. Then you and I walk
in. You're my best friend, bro. After everything we've
gone through together, it just felt right to have you beside me."

"I'll be there." Benjamin stood up and looked down
over the balcony. Piper was walking the police officer
out. He couldn't see where Dominic had gone. "I promise. Whatever it takes."

Otherwise he'd never be able to forgive himself.

Piper looked up. Benjamin was standing alone on
the balcony above her. He slipped a cell phone into his
pocket and then started down the stairs toward her.

"Where did everybody go?" he asked.

"The police finished up their report," she said. "They
already have someone trying to match the description
you gave them of Kodiak and they'll apply for a search
warrant to go through his phone. They're on the look-
out for your truck and will also try to have someone
drive by The Downs a couple of times in the night, just
to make sure everything's okay and to show anyone
who might be prowling around that they're watching.
Dominic's gone home to grab a few things. Now that
the guests have moved out he's taking a second-floor
suite for tonight, so that you and I have another person
here for backup."

Benjamin dropped down on the couch beside her.
"So you guessed that I'm going nowhere tonight."

"I had a hunch." The back of her hand brushed the
back of his. Then she folded her hands in her lap. "Are
you okay?"

"Depends how you define *okay*." He looked so tired
she was amazed he was still standing upright. "I have

no passport, no truck, no clothes, there's another snow-storm outside, the bridge to Manitoulin Island is clos-ing tonight due to ice and my sister is getting married tomorrow." He shook his head in what she assumed was exasperation. "But you and I are both safe, and it could be a whole lot worse. So, sure, all things consid-ered, I'm okay."

"Yeah, I'm pretty much the same," she said. "The barn has collapsed, taking the tree we chopped down and the Christmas decorations with it. I have no idea what I'm going to do about Christmas Eve at The Downs, since we obviously can't hold it in the barn now. Kodiak, Alpha and the blonde who broke into my room are all still on the loose. According to police, it sounds like no one's heard from Charlotte since the night she trashed The Downs. It's like she evaporated into thin air. As far as the police can tell she did a com-plete disappearing act."

Which did not bode well for either finding her or stopping those now after her.

"Maybe she changed her identity," Benjamin said. "Especially if she was trying to escape Alpha. Do they have any idea why the barn collapsed?"

"Yup, but you won't believe it, because I barely be-lieve it myself. Someone walked around on the barn roof and tried to break into the top of the chimney."

He blinked. "You're joking."

"No word of a lie." She ran both hands through her hair and let it fall. "The stupid thing is I thought I saw something up there when we were driving in to drop off the tree. I just never realized it could be a person. But that's the theory based on the footprints, broken branches and what they could piece together. They actually found a sledgehammer in the rubble. Looks like someone climbed up, took a few swings at the brick. They tried to climb back down, but the branch broke and everything caved in. They fell through but obviously managed to crawl out while we were still buried, and then stole your truck, I'm guessing."

"Did you check the brick? I think I heard her say something about bricks to that guy."

One of Alpha's angry texts floated through her mind. But that couldn't be the "brick" Alpha was talking about. Could it? After all, whoever trashed the barn also took a couple of swipes at the fireplace and stopped when they hit the heavy wall of concrete Uncle Des had poured in.

Benjamin's mouth gaped. "You're telling me that someone was actually climbing around on your barn roof, trying to break into the chimney with a sledgehammer?"

"Yup." She nodded. "The police said they'd check The Downs's roof for footprints, too, but they figure it's too steep to climb on."

"Do you realize how ridiculous that sounds? They could have been killed. We could have been killed. I shouldn't be finding this funny."

Benjamin looked on the cusp of bursting into laughter. But Piper was almost ready to cry.

"It's ridiculous. I know!" She threw her hands up in the air. "It's too absurd for words. Six years ago I try to do the nice thing and let some girl I'm sharing an apartment with come visit The Downs because she's curious about the rumors of its Prohibition history. Instead, she sneaks out to kiss some handsome young man in the woods, robs my family and our guests, and destroys pretty much every special handmade Christmas ornament we have. And why? I don't know! Now my aunt is ill, I'm saving every cent I can for renovating this place and suddenly she's back to wreck my life even more spectacularly than before. Only I haven't *seen* her. Not specifically. All I've seen is a masked blonde girl, who could be Charlotte. Thanks to the phone you inadvertently picked up after fighting Kodiak, we now have pretty strong confirmation he was sent here by Charlotte's former boyfriend. But why Alpha is looking for Charlotte here after all this time is still a giant mystery, because as far as I can tell, *she's not here*! And there's nothing I can do!"

That was probably more of an outburst than Benjamin had ever heard from her before. But, while she might have been born in England and raised by a couple who were strong believers in staying calm and carrying on, with everything that had been mounting the past couple of days it was getting harder and harder not to throw her metaphorical hockey gloves down on the ice and pound something.

She took a deep breath, afraid she already knew the answer before she asked the question. "What happens to your flight to Australia?"

He sighed. "I don't know. Whoever stole my truck now has my passport. I don't know how fast I'll be able to get a new one, but it doesn't look good. Worst-case scenario, I wait days or weeks for the passport to arrive, book a new flight, get over there as soon I can and figure out how I'm going to join the charity sail after it starts."

He was sitting so close to her on the couch now she caught his scent—like the forest after a rain, like spices, like comfort. If she moved her body just an inch they would be touching. Shadows from the flickering flames danced along the lines of his jaw. Piper ached to reach up and feel the softness of his beard under her fingertips, to brush her lips along the soft skin where it met his cheek.

No. She'd kissed him once and that had been a mistake. They couldn't let it happen again. She leaped up. "I have some mulled cider in the pantry. I'm going to go heat it up over the stove."

A question flickered in his eyes, but he didn't follow her.

The kitchen was dark. She walked through the narrow room and headed for the pantry.

Lord, please help Benjamin catch his flight. I never thought I'd say this, but I need him to leave. The next goodbye has to be the final one, no matter what. I can't keep having my heart yanked up and down like a yo-yo anymore.

She opened the pantry door and pulled the cord for the light out of habit before remembering the power was still out and they were reliant on a generator. She stepped in and ran her hands along the jars and cans, feeling for the cloth-wrapped cider lid.

Something moved in the darkness. Then before she could barely make a sound, a gloved hand clamped tightly over her lips and the tip of a knife brushed against her neck.

"Don't move!" the man whispered. "Or I'll have to kill you."

THIRTEEN

A crash came from the kitchen.

"Hey, everything okay in there? You need a hand?" Benjamin glanced over his shoulder. He thought he heard a muffled sound but couldn't make out any words. He stood up. "Hang on, I'll come hold a flashlight—"

The words froze in his throat as Piper walked, slowly and awkwardly into the living room. A black-gloved hand was clamped over her mouth and the tip of a jagged kitchen knife was pressed into the soft flesh at the base of her throat.

Oh Lord, help me save her.

She took another step toward him and it was only then he saw her attacker. The man was about Piper's height but had an athletic build. He wore a shiny red ski jacket and a striped balaclava that hid his face, but not enough to hide the bruised eye and bloody lip.

Not Kodiak. Not Blondie.

Was he face-to-face with Alpha?

Benjamin focused his gaze directly on Piper. "Don't worry. It's going to be okay."

"Don't talk to her!" the man snapped. "Just tell me where I can find what I'm looking for or someone's going to get hurt!

Piper's hands rose in front of her. "Okay. We hear you."

But her eyes met Benjamin's, determined, fearless.

He took a step forward, praying for an opportunity, his limbs tense and ready to strike. "We have no idea where Charlotte is."

"What?" The masked man's head snapped toward Benjamin. "Who's Charlotte?"

But the final syllable froze in the masked man's throat.

Piper swiftly grabbed his wrist with both hands and pulled it out in front of her face. For a second the blade reflected in her eyes before she twisted his wrist, wrenching the knife from his grasp.

He screamed in pain, dropping the knife to the floor.

She tossed him over her shoulder.

The masked man landed on his back on the floor and lay there, staring up at her with bulging eyes. She still hadn't let go of his wrist.

Then Piper tossed her hair and looked at Benjamin, fire flashing in her eyes.

Benjamin's mouth went dry.

He couldn't remember ever seeing anything stronger, braver or more beautiful in his entire life.

"Got the knife?" she asked.

"Yeah." Benjamin picked it up and held it out firmly, just enough to show the intruder that even though Piper had the situation covered he was more than happy to step in as needed.

Only then did Piper release her grip just enough to let the man rise to his knees.

He spat on the floor. "You broke my arm."

"Probably just sprained. We'll call an ambulance

when we call the police." Benjamin reached down and yanked off the ski mask.

It was Gavin.

Benjamin almost laughed. The same arrogant jerk who'd stood in this kitchen just this morning insulting him had just threatened Piper at knifepoint, and was now down on his knees, his bruised and bloody face glaring defiantly at them.

Benjamin hoped the disgust he was feeling showed clearly in his eyes.

"Who sent you here?" Piper turned on Gavin. "Was it Alpha? Why do they think Charlotte is at The Downs?"

A snarl passed Gavin's lips. "I told you, I don't know anyone named Charlotte and I've never heard of Alpha. I don't know what's going on here any more than you do!"

Benjamin snorted. Even though Gavin had spit the words out with so much anger and frustration it was likely he'd convinced himself they were true. But Benjamin wasn't about to listen to the hotheaded liar and sneak who'd assaulted Piper claim that he was the victim.

"Well, I hope whatever you're after is worth losing your legal career for. If you even are a lawyer." Piper turned to Benjamin. "There's a phone behind you on the counter. If you call 911, they should hopefully be able to get us through to the right officer for our case."

"Agreed." Benjamin reached for the phone.

"Wait! Please!" Sweat was pouring down Gavin's face. "Don't call the police. Just get someone to take me to the hospital. Or call a taxi and I'll make my own way there. Okay, okay, so I don't have my own law firm yet. But I did just pass the bar exam and I'll agree

not to sue you, or press charges for assaulting me or...
or for the fact I fell through the roof of your obviously
unstable barn. We can all just chalk this up to one big
misunderstanding and go on with our lives."

Fury built at the back of Benjamin's neck, tighten-
ing his shoulders and pushing through his voice with
so much force. "You *attacked* Piper! You broke into
her home. You put a knife to her throat. Not to mention
vandalizing the power generator, taking a sledgehammer to the chimney of her barn, and conspiring with
some creep with a bear tattoo who choked her at the
barn last night—"

Gavin's hands rose higher. "I don't know anything
about any of that!"

Benjamin's eyebrow rose.

"Okay, yeah," Gavin conceded. "I did threaten Piper
with a knife right now and I did sort of trespass on the
roof of her barn, and hit the chimney with a sledgehammer. But in my defense, I didn't know her barn roof was
so weak. And I didn't touch her generator, or do any of
those other things. And I only threatened her right now
because I was getting so desperate and frustrated. I was
hired by somebody to find something, okay?"

"Hired to find what?" Benjamin demanded.

"I don't really know."

"Who hired you? Was it Alpha?"

"I don't know! Look, I'm kind of a subcontractor.
Trisha hired me." His whole body seemed to deflate and
sink into the floor. "Trisha's not really my wife. She's
definitely not a lawyer and she's only twenty-two. She
came into the legal clinic where I was working and offered me five hundred dollars to go away with her over
Christmas."

Benjamin snorted. Gavin was claiming Trisha had paid him to come to The Downs with her and pretend to be her husband? "Really? That's the story you're going with now?"

Benjamin reached for the phone again.

"Wait! Look, I'm telling the truth!" Gavin yelled. "I met her a few months ago. She seemed to be in some kind of trouble with a really bad boyfriend and I'm a nice guy, so I found out her contact details and tried to keep in touch with her afterward. I kept texting and asking her out every now and then over the next few months, trying to build a rapport. She kept saying no and telling me to leave her alone. Then all of a sudden she offers me money to go away with her over Christmas and pretend to be her husband. Should've known it was too good to be true. I hadn't even realized she was pregnant and she wouldn't let me get anywhere near her. But I needed the money and thought she might've started liking me. But when we got here she basically just hid in the room and got me to do all kinds of stupid stuff for her."

Okay, that much Benjamin could believe. If Trisha had been looking to use someone—for whatever reason—Gavin might have seemed both arrogant and foolish enough to be a dupe.

"Did Trisha have anyone else working for her?" Piper loosened her grip on Gavin. "Or was she working for anyone?"

"I don't know." Gavin frowned and cradled his sore arm. "Her story kept changing. At first she told me she was here looking for a person. But then the person wasn't here and suddenly she says we need to go through the Christmas decorations in the barn and take a look inside the barn chimney. And why the chimney? I don't know. It was as if her connection with reality was totally slipping. Or maybe someone was just giving her really weird directions. She was texting someone a lot. All I know is I got tired of being her lackey and began to worry I was never going to see my money. Especially after you kicked us out. Falling through the barn was the last straw. So I decided to take matters into my own hands. Figured Piper might know what was going on."

As ridiculous as this sounded, it was also consistent with what he'd seen on Kodiak's phone. So that made multiple people under Alpha's command. Benjamin met Piper's eyes.

"I'm pretty sure Trisha was getting instructions from Alpha, too," she said, "and that she's scared witless of him."

Yeah, he could see that, too. But Uncle Des had seen Charlotte kissing a strong, young man. If neither Kodiak nor Gavin were Alpha, they were running out of suspects. The only other person he'd met in town who met that description was the mechanic.

"Where is Trisha now?" Benjamin asked.

"Where's Benjamin's truck and stuff?" Piper spoke almost at the same time.

"I have no idea." Gavin's shoulders rose and fell. "After I climbed out of the barn, I told Trisha I was done. So she stole your truck and split, because it was my vehicle we'd come up in. No girl, no matter how cute, is worth that much trouble, am I right?" Gavin grinned, foolishly. "But I have her cell phone number and I really can't afford any legal problems at this stage of my career. So, how about you help me figure out what she was looking for, and then help me find it, and I'll cut you in for a share of the money to help you renovate this old dump. What do you say?"

Piper's eyes rolled. Benjamin just looked down at the phone and dialed.

"911. What's your emergency?"

"Hi, this is Benjamin Duff calling from The Downs—"

Gavin shouted. Benjamin turned, just in time to see the man lunge for Piper's legs in an apparent last-minute attempt to escape justice. Piper swung, her elbow catching Gavin square in the jaw. He crumpled to the floor. Benjamin shook his head. The whole thing had taken less than a couple of seconds.

"Hello?" The 911 operator was back in his ear.

"There's been a break-in. We need police and an ambulance. The intruder threatened the proprietor with a knife and clearly underestimated who he was dealing with."

Gavin was taken away in an ambulance, all the while demanding loudly that the police go find and arrest Trisha instead, because everything was entirely her fault. The same flurry of police cars and people in uniform that had become all too common a sight at The Downs in the past two days came and left as quickly as a winter snow squall. By ten thirty, Piper and the dog had gone upstairs to her room, Dominic had settled into the large suite Tobias had vacated, and despite having a more than adequate four-poster bed on the second floor to himself, Benjamin once again found himself tossing and turning on the living-room couch.

He couldn't sleep.

Snow buffeted gently against the towering windows. A thirty-five-foot ceiling vaulted high above his head.

The expansive room twisted and turned at the edges into nooks, crannies and alcoves. He lost track trying to count the number of walls the room even had. No wonder people suspected The Downs had been used as a hidden speakeasy or some other criminal enterprise with illegal alcohol and dirty money. Everything about this house projected mystery, suspense and intrigue.

He could also see why Piper's uncle and aunt loved the place so much and hoped to live out their last days here.

The fire was burning down to embers and the box of wood beside the fireplace was running low. He grabbed his coat and started for the woodpile out back. The grandfather clock chimed midnight. His footstep paused. He was down to eighteen hours to his sister's wedding.

Christmas Eve had arrived.

Not that it showed in the space around him. The lights Piper had strung outside hadn't come back to life since the power had gone out yesterday, and there wasn't so much as a string of tinsel or a sprig of holly inside The Downs.

He held out the battery-powered lantern in front of him as he walked. The track pants and T-shirt he'd borrowed from Dominic were a size too big, but the clothes were warm enough against the cold. Thick white snow fell down from the sky, brushing his skin and sticking to his beard.

Lantern light ran over the large kindling box. It was about three feet tall and five feet long. The idea of anyone being cruel enough to lock Piper inside it burned through his veins like fire. No, he didn't judge Piper for relegating Christmas Eve at The Downs to the now-damaged barn. If anything, he admired her all the more for taking on the community event in her aunt's place. He couldn't blame her for not filling her living room with memories of Christmas, either. It was as if someone else's cruelty and malice had taken even the happy symbols of the holiday and smashed them to bits.

He filled his arms with small branches and kindling. The remnants of the broken hockey stick from when Piper had fought off Blondie last night had been tossed on top of the woodpile. In fact, there was more than one broken hockey stick, a broken paddle and half a cross-country ski scattered among the logs and branches. He chuckled. Yeah, the Piper he'd gone running, kayaking and sailing with that summer had been strong, daring and utterly fearless. But not always easy on either herself or her sports equipment.

The dull ache he'd felt in his chest at the memory of Piper's smile strengthened to pain. It was like hunger pangs for something that he couldn't quite put a name to. He'd thought the pain was bad that hot summer night when Piper had said goodbye and walked out of the restaurant, and that swinging by to drop off Harry would somehow put it to rest. Instead, it had just kept growing stronger every moment they'd spent together.

He turned his face to the sky and prayed aloud.

"Lord, You've got to know how awesome Piper is. I trust that You want an amazing life for her, just as much as I do. It was incredible the way she took Gavin down. Right now everything inside my heart is aching to help her, save her...or even just to give her a reason to smile this Christmas. But I've never felt so helpless and I don't know where to start."

His eyes slid over the tree line as a memory filled his mind. A year and a half ago, he'd picked up his reporter friend Jack from the police station on the island. This was long before Jack was his sister's fiancé or had even admitted to himself how perfect he and Meg were together. Benjamin had been driving and drinking coffee. Jack had been ranting about how impossible his situation was, almost on the verge of falling apart. A serial killer was stalking Meg. Jack was in trouble with the police and about to lose his job. And Benjamin had turned to the reporter, told him some camping story about a nonexistent bear, and then said something like, "I didn't ask what you can't do. I asked what you're gonna do."

Now here he was standing in a snowstorm, freezing his feet off, worrying about everything he couldn't fix. To be fair there was whole lot he couldn't do right now. But figuring out what he could still do wasn't a bad place to start.

He grabbed the broken hockey stick.

Piper woke with a start and stared into the darkness, unable to tell if she really had just heard a noise downstairs or if it had just been an echo of the nightmare she could barely remember. Silence filled her ears, interrupted only by the sound of Harry snoring at her feet. The clock read six thirty in the morning. It was Christmas Eve. The world was still pitch-black outside her window, but she might as well get up.

Her mind urged her to start making plans about how she was going to salvage the Christmas Eve potluck now that she'd lost the barn. But that would have to wait until after some coffee. She threw on jeans and pulled on a hockey jersey. Her feet dragged across the floor. Harry didn't even follow, just stretched out on the full length of her bed. Guess that meant that he wasn't bothered by whatever she might have heard. She felt her way down the stairs in the darkness, pushed the door open and stepped out onto the second-floor landing.

"Hang on! Don't move." Benjamin's voice floated up to her through the darkness. "Just wait one second."

"Okay…" What was going on? She couldn't see a thing.

"All right," he said. "This isn't much, I know. But my goal was to come up with something totally different and unique, that you probably hadn't ever seen in The Downs before. And seeing as I didn't manage to get you a Christmas present, I wanted to leave you with something."

She heard the whirring of the windup flashlight. The outline of a tall Christmas tree slowly came to life in the gentle glow of white fairy lights. She walked down the stairs watching as the lights grew brighter. A tall, handmade wooden Christmas tree stood beside the fireplace. A long, worn board formed the trunk. Bits of wood, hockey sticks and pieces of a canoe paddle formed the branches. Intricate crisscrossing twigs formed the star on the top. Christmas lights weaved through and around makeshift branches, plugged into the power outlet of Benjamin's windup flashlight.

His eyes met hers, hopeful, questioning. "So, what do you think?"

"It's incredible." She felt a smile tug at the corner of her lips. "I don't know what to say."

"I'm glad you like it." His eyes drew her in deeper. "I

found a toolbox in the garage and pulled the wood from the woodpile. I know it's not much and I figured if you didn't like it, it would be easy enough to dismantle—"

"Stop it." She ran across the floor toward him. "You're being hard on yourself and you don't need to." She slipped her arms around his waist and hugged him. "I love it. Thank you. It's too beautiful for words."

"Well, you're beautiful. After everything you've been through I wouldn't blame you if you hated Christmas. I just wanted to leave you with something to hopefully help build a happy memory." His arms encircled her shoulders, his fingers locking behind her back. The tree lights began to slowly dim again. "You're the kindest, most caring, pluckiest person I've ever met. Someone came along and stepped all over your Christmas memories and you just rolled your shoulders back and carried on making sure the holiday was still special for other people. I just hope you know that I'd do whatever I could to make sure you had a really amazing Christmas."

Then don't leave. Don't go to Australia. Her cheek pressed against his chest as the words she didn't dare let herself say filled her heart. *Forget about your boat. Forget about sailing the world. Just stay here with me and help me run this old, boring bed-and-breakfast in the middle of nowhere. I know it's selfish to even think of asking you to give up your dreams. Because you're right about this not making me happy. I wish my aunt Cass wasn't sick, that The Downs wasn't broke and that I could just pack up and leave here, too. But I can't. I'm needed here.*

So, I wish what made you happy was being here, in The Downs, with me.

Because right now the only thing that makes me truly happy here is you.

No, she wouldn't say that. She'd never say anything even close to that. Because the only thing that hurt worse than the thought of Benjamin leaving was knowing she sent him off with a heavy heart. Whenever he managed to catch that plane, the last thing she wanted him carrying with him was the weight of knowing just how sad she'd be.

She took in a deep breath and breathed him in. She memorized the feel of his arms around her shoulders and the scent of him filling her lungs. Her eyes closed. Then she felt his lips brush her forehead. His fingertips lifted up her chin right before she felt the sweetness and scruff of his lips finding hers.

The kiss lingered, as naturally and tenderly as breath filling their lungs.

Then Piper stepped back. Benjamin did, too.

"How soon do you leave?" she asked.

"Soon." Benjamin ran his hand over his face. "Very soon."

She didn't know which one of them had initiated the kiss or which one of them had stopped it. But maybe it didn't matter. They were like two of the little magnet dogs she had as a child. They kept pulling together and pushing apart, the two of them trapped in an invisible orbit.

The pale gray light of winter morning began to fill the windows above their head.

"I want to make sure the bridge has been reopened and that you're ready for your party tonight," Benjamin said. "But I hope to leave by ten at the latest. Do you know what you're going to do about tonight yet?"

"No, not yet." She dropped into a chair by the window and pulled a blanket over her knees. For a moment she just sat and let her eyes run over the intricate work he'd done on the makeshift Christmas tree. Benjamin crossed the floor, sat down on the carpet and leaned his broad shoulder against her legs.

"Aunt Cass used to host Christmas Eve in this room when I was little. They'd push all the furniture back, set up a string of potluck dishes down the kitchen counter and let everyone come through and feed themselves. It was a big, happy, chaotic mess." She glanced up. "People used to sit on the second-floor balcony with their feet dangling down. Sixteen-year-olds. Sixty-year-olds. It was a madhouse."

He looked up at her face. "Sounds amazing."

"Oh, it was. But it was hard, too, because I was an only child, and this was my home and I never liked having all these people galloping through my space. I'm hardly an extrovert like Aunt Cass. Sometimes I wonder if she moved the whole thing out to the barn because she suspected it would be easier on me that way." She sighed. "I love knowing that I'm helping my uncle and aunt keep their home. I love knowing I'm part of something that's done so much for this community. But I don't love the chaos of it all."

"All tacking, no sailing?" Benjamin asked.

"Lots of loudly heralding angels and banging drummer boys. No 'Silent Night'."

Feet padded above them and she looked up to see Harry making his way down the staircase. Benjamin got up and disappeared into the kitchen. She heard him pouring kibble into the dog bowl, then he reemerged, a cup of coffee in each hand.

"You know how we did all that wilderness stuff together this summer?" He handed her a cup. "Well, I don't do all that with just anyone. Not for fun. Most people are either too shy or too loud. But you've got a really good combination of getting things done and knowing how to just exist in the moment and let a guy think." He sat down beside her. "You're the most comfortable person I've ever been around. I think you'd be awesome to go on a sailing voyage with. I'm going to miss you so much, Piper, you have no idea."

Her fingers slid through his. "I'm going to miss you, too."

"Hey! Good morning!" A loud, cheerful voice floated from above them. Dominic was standing on the second-story balcony. The wannabe cop strode down the stairs. "Do I smell coffee?"

"Yes." Piper stood quickly. "Benjamin was kind enough to make some."

"Awesome." Dominic smiled broadly. "Whoa, that hockey tree is something else! Did Benjamin make that?"

Piper ran her hands up and down her arms, trying to brush away the shivers Benjamin's words had left on her skin. "Yes, he's quite the craftsman."

Dominic clasped his hands together like a fighter ready to enter the ring. "Now, Pips, tell me what I can do to help you pull off Christmas Eve at The Downs. You want me to start calling around to church and school halls? You want me to round up volunteers and see who's still able to get here? I can get my whole extended family worth of cousins, plus the youth group of my church here in minutes."

"Thank you. Get some coffee into you and then we'll

make a game plan." Piper's gaze ran over Benjamin's tree. "I think we're going to hold Christmas Eve here, in this room. It will be crowded and mean some last-minute adjustments. Especially if the power doesn't come back on. But people can bring backup generators and hot plates, and we can light candles. We can make it work." She felt Dominic nod his assent, but she only had eyes for Benjamin. "It's been a long time since we've held Christmas here. I think it's time to bring it home."

By the time the clock chimed nine thirty, The Downs was standing room only. Good to his word, Dominic had not only rounded up his entire extended family, but teenagers from three different youth groups, many of whom had brought friends and family members of their own. Boxes of donated Christmas decorations filled the garage. Uncle Des had organized a minibus of seniors from Silver Halls, many of whom were now seated around the dining room table teaching the youngsters how to make decorations. Aunt Cass had hit the phones and was getting a faithful crew of volunteer cooks to amend their menus. The driveway was being plowed to make more space for cars. A bonfire was coming together on the wide expanse of snow between the house and hill. Garlands of freshly cut pine branches and bows were being strung from the balcony railing above her. Even Tobias had turned up after hearing the news from someone at the local bookshop. The plump professor was now directing a makeshift Christmas choir on the staircase. And every few moments the front doorbell rang with loans of plates and cutlery, candles, battery lamps and backup generators.

Piper stood in the living room and watched the hustle of energy and life flow around her.

Lord, I had no idea this was possible. Just... Thank You.

"You doing okay?" A comforting hand brushed her shoulder, as Benjamin's voice rumbled softly in her ear.

"Yeah. I'm good." She stepped backward into his chest and pulled his arm around her shoulders. "You're going now, right?"

He'd changed back into the clothes he'd been wearing the day before. He'd hand-washed them and gotten out the dirt, but there was no helping the gaping holes and grease stains in his jeans.

"Yeah, I'm sorry. I have to. My sister's getting married in a little over eight hours, and I've got a seven-hour drive ahead of me. But call me if you need anything. Or if you can't reach me because I'm out of cell phone range, call my sister and leave a message there. I left her number on the pad beside your phone."

"It's okay." She turned around inside his arms and his strong hands brushed the small of her back. "You go be where you need to be. I'm going to be just fine. Promise."

They were standing in the middle of the living room, while people rushed around and chaos reigned around them. But, in that moment, it was as if nothing else existed but his eyes on her face and his arms hugging her goodbye.

"I wish you could come with me," he said softly. "And I wish I could stay to help with Christmas Eve."

"Well, I don't wish you could stay." *Not at The Downs. Not forever. Because it's not who you are. It's not where you belong or what would make you happy.* "You've waited all your life for this trip. So you go. Just say goodbye, hug me tight and then go."

"It might take a few days before I leave. I still have

to sort my passport and rebook my flight. If I have a bit more time—"

"Just go. Don't look back. I don't want to have to keep saying goodbye to you over and over again."

She closed her eyes and felt the scruff of his beard on her cheek. Then his lips hovered over hers.

"Hey! Isn't that Benji Duff?" a young voice shouted from somewhere behind her. "Hey, dude, look! I think that's the snowmobile crash guy! Yo! Benji! What did it feel like to almost die?"

Benjamin kissed her on the top of her head. Then he stepped back. "Goodbye, Piper."

She took in a deep breath and let it out slowly. When she opened her eyes, he was gone. She blinked hard. No, she wasn't going to cry.

"Piper, honey? Can you come here a second?" Aunt Cass's voice cut through the noise inside the house. "I was just telling people about the wonderful paper decorations you made for us years ago. I was wondering if you wanted to show us."

Piper nodded. "Sure thing."

She suspected her aunt was trying to give her a distraction, something to keep her hands busy while she calmed the raging battle of emotions inside her heart. For that, she was grateful.

She walked over to the dining-room table and sat down. Her hands reached, unseeing, for a scrap of newspaper and tore it into triangular strips. Tear, fold, weave. Set aside. Grab a new sheet. Tear, fold, weave. If she just keep her hands moving, let the pain move through her like a river, she'd be fine.

"Hey, who taught you to make paper stars?"

She looked up. Dominic was standing above her on

the stairs. His eyebrow rose. Oddly, he looked more than a little troubled. It was worrying.

"Nobody taught me to do this. It's just some craft I invented as a kid."

Aunt Cass patted her arm. "She made a huge, beautiful newspaper star for me this way when she was about eight or nine. Used to sit on top of my tree." Her aunt's eyes darkened. "It was one of the things that we lost that Christmas Eve six years ago."

Dominic's face paled. As Piper watched, his hand rose to his mouth. Then he turned and darted up the stairs.

What on earth?

Piper jumped up and followed after him. She caught up to him part way up the stairs. "What's up with you?"

"I'm so sorry, Pips! I think I did a really stupid thing. But believe me, I didn't know!"

FOURTEEN

Dominic clenched his hands. Whatever he'd done had left him so agitated it almost frightened her. She glanced through the large front windows. Benjamin was standing in the driveway, saying goodbye to Uncle Des. By the look of things, two teenaged boys had followed them out. One of them was now trying to get Benjamin to autograph his hat.

Dominic edged his way up the staircase, weaving his way around the staircase choir. He disappeared into his guest room.

She rapped on the door. "Look, Dominic. I'm your friend. Whatever you did, whatever you're upset about, you can tell me."

There was a long pause. Then the cop-in-training opened the suite door. His shoulders hunched. "I kissed someone I shouldn't have kissed."

That's it? Piper's gaze ran down to the mass of people teeming below. Her friend was having a crisis, on Christmas Eve, over an ill-advised romantic interlude? "Who did you kiss?"

Dominic's gaze dropped to his feet. "Charlotte."

"You kissed Charlotte?" Piper's voice rose to a shriek.

Dominic nodded miserably. "I'm sorry. I didn't know what kind of person she was."

How could he have possibly kept a secret like this from her?

She ushered him into the room. "When was this? Recently? Is she nearby? When are you seeing her again?"

"No, of course not! It was six years ago!"

Piper's shoulders sank.

Dominic's gaze dropped to his feet. "We hit it off the night you brought her here. But she told me we could only be friends in secret and you could never know. We used to meet in the trees. She had this terrible former boyfriend she was really scared of. She was afraid he was going to come to The Downs and cause trouble. One night I was comforting her. Then the next thing I knew, she was kissing me."

She probably shouldn't be surprised, after all this lined up with everything she already knew.

"I didn't know she was going to rob you," Dominic said, his voice rising. "She said she was going away for a while and that I shouldn't try to find her, but that she'd come back as soon as she could. She gave me this beautiful newspaper star on Christmas Eve and told me she'd made it for me because I was such a nice guy. I had no idea she'd stolen it from you. Honest, Piper! If I had, I'd have made sure you got it back. She made me promise I'd keep it forever. But I was so embarrassed after everything that happened I just hid it in a box in the cupboard because I thought it was just some random Christmas thing."

Piper ran her hand through her hair. He'd been

only about nineteen at the time. She couldn't begin to imagine the turmoil his emotions must have been in. "Where's the star now?"

He looked around the room. "In one of the boxes of stuff in my car. That's why I ran to my room right now. I thought I might've brought it in. But it must still be in the trunk of the car."

In Dominic's car? The car that he'd lent to Benjamin to drive to Manitoulin Island? She ran to the window and looked out just in time to see Benjamin shut the driver's-side door. She squeezed Dominic's shoulder. "It's okay. Please don't worry about it. Charlotte made a fool out of a lot of us. I'm going to run and try to grab Benjamin before he leaves."

A handmade newspaper star from her childhood might be a small thing. But it would still be one special thing she could do for Aunt Cass. She dashed down the stairs, grabbing her coat as she sprinted out the front door.

"Benjamin!" The car was pulling away. She chased it down the driveway, waving both hands over her head. "Hey, wait!"

But the small red car pulled onto the road and disappeared.

She went back to the house and shrugged off her coat, feeling like a balloon whose air was slowly seeping out. One of his sister's friends would be driving the car back for Dominic a few days after the wedding. She could get the star back then.

But, watching Benjamin drive away while she'd run after him waving frantically caused a pain that stung her chest.

True, he hadn't noticed she was there. Yet, she'd really

wanted to remember the other goodbye, the final one of this Christmas. The one where she was strong, composed and encouraged him to go. Not one where she chased after him frantically, even if she was only after a sentimental newspaper Christmas craft.

"Hey, did anyone bring some string? I'm running low and wanted to weave some bows through the banister." The request came from the teenaged boy standing above on the balcony.

"Absolutely," Piper called up. "Pretty sure I've got both fishing wire and a roll of twine downstairs."

Her feet echoed down the stairs into the empty basement. A cold breeze brushed her body as the door swung shut behind her. She paused a moment and let her eyes to adjust to the darkness. A few moments alone to compose herself probably wasn't a bad idea. Besides she'd always liked the cellar. It was crowded, cluttered and comforting, far too small for a house the size of The Downs, and full of hidden nooks and crannies. Mysterious and peaceful all at once.

She heard something crash in the darkness. She glanced up, just in time to see a flash of blond hair peeking out from under a navy ski mask. Blondie!

"Hey! Stop!" Piper dashed after her.

Blondie climbed onto a low shelf and then leaped through the open basement window.

If the woman thought after all this Piper would let her just run, she had another thought coming. Piper sprinted across the basement floor, dove through the window and crawled out into the snow. Ahead of her she could see a slim figure running for the trees.

Nice try, Blondie, but nobody outruns an athlete on her home turf.

Piper dashed after her through the snow. When Blondie hesitated, Piper lunged, catching the slender woman around the knees and throwing her into the snow.

Blondie struggled wildly, but Piper flipped her over and pinned her down hard.

She yanked the ski mask off, taking the fake blond wig along with it.

She stared down at the thin, short-haired brunette lying in the snow.

Trisha.

So, the blond hair had been fake. Did that mean... She glanced at the woman's slender waist. Trisha's pregnant belly had been fake, too. Piper shook her head. Benjamin had been right when he said the right clothes could do a lot to disguise the shape of someone's body.

"Where is Alpha?" Piper said. "What on earth has he gotten you into?"

The windshield wipers cut back and forth past Benjamin's eyes. Less than an hour after leaving Piper's he was caught inside an unexpected snow squall. He'd taken Des's advice and stuck to empty back roads instead of the main highway and, according to the snippets of traffic and weather he was able to catch on the intermittent radio, he'd made the right choice. But still the car was crawling forward and the snow was so thick it was practically a whiteout.

Dominic's car was tiny. Way lighter on the road than the comforting bulk of Benjamin's four-wheel drive truck. Even with the front seat slid all the way back Benjamin could barely make room for his cramped legs. The boxes Dominic had left in the back made visibility even harder. He'd driven his sister's hatchback from time to time, when circumstances demanded it, but why any grown man would voluntarily drive such a small car was beyond him.

A sudden pang of sadness nicked his heart.

He really missed his truck.

Along with his torn bag, his clothes, his passport—and the sense of certainty he'd had in his heart just two days earlier.

He glanced in the rearview mirror. Was that another set of headlights behind him? He couldn't even remember the last time he'd been passed by another vehicle. There was no music on the radio, nothing in the tape deck and nothing to see out the window but an endless stream of white in all directions.

Nothing to distract him from thoughts of Piper.

Nothing to keep the smell of her hair, the touch of her hand, or the curve of her smile from taking over the corners of his mind and driving him crazy. How was he ever going to manage missing her this much? How soon would it be until thoughts of her faded away?

His cell phone started to ring from its mount on the dashboard. He pushed the button. "Hello?"

"Benji?" Meg's voice echoed through the tiny car.

"Hey, sis! All is well. I'm still on my way. At this rate I'll be there by five thirty."

He heard Meg breathe a prayer of relief under her breath.

His eyes rose to the rearview mirror again. Those headlights were growing closer.

Was someone actually going to try to pass him in weather like this?

"You've got to speak louder," he said. "I'm using the

phone hands-free. In fact, I should hang up soon. It's like driving through a milk shake."

"Okay. Can you send your GPS location to my phone, so I have a sense where you're at?"

"Sorry, I forgot." Fortunately he had a map function installed on his phone that not only kept track of where in the world he was, but emailed it to others. Meg was already preprogrammed in. All it took was the push of a button. "Done. You should be able to see my whole route. But my exact location may not be that accurate, though, as I keep blipping in and out of cell-tower range." The headlights behind him now filled his rearview mirror. "I've gotta go. See you soon."

"Drive safe."

"Will do." He hung up and gripped the steering wheel with both hands.

The vehicle behind was far too close for his liking now. It was big, too. A large, old pickup truck apparently being driven by the kind of person who thought they owned the road. The truck inched closer.

Hey, buddy, back it up, okay. There's no reason we can't share. Benjamin slowed even more and nudged the car over to the side of the road, giving as much room as possible for the other vehicle to pass. The truck pulled alongside him. Benjamin glanced toward the other vehicle and gave what he hoped looked like a friendly wave toward the tinted window. *Just go ahead and pass. This doesn't have to be a race. We've all got places to be this Christmas.*

The truck didn't pass. The truck's passenger window rolled down. Benjamin's blood froze as he looked over into the cold dead eyes of the man who'd threatened Piper and come hunting for Charlotte.

Kodiak raised his gun and fired.

Benjamin's window exploded inward. The bullet barely missed him before coming to rest in the passenger-side door. Glass filled the front seat.

Benjamin gripped the wheel tightly. He forced his gaze on the road ahead and his heart to the God above.

Help me, Lord. Help me. I can't outrun Kodiak in this car. I can't escape him. I—

Another gunshot.

This one clanged somewhere on the body of the car.

The prayer choked in Benjamin's throat. His mind froze. He was trapped.

Just like that moment, almost sixteen years ago, when he'd seen the headlights of that transport truck barreling through the snow toward him and had been convinced he was going to die.

Another shot exploded his front tire and the car spun off the road. It crashed through the barrier and careened down the hill.

He rolled, side over side, through the trees. Then slammed to a stop upside down as an air bag exploded in his face.

The seat belt snapped him back against the seat holding him upside down in the overturned car.

The sound of the horn filled his ears.

He started to pray. *Lord, please don't let me die this way. Not on Meg's wedding day. Not on Christmas Eve. Piper needs...*

Darkness swam before his eyes. He could feel the deep pull of unconsciousness at the corner of his mind now, like an old enemy waiting to strike. He gritted his teeth and tried to resume his prayer but he couldn't shake the feeling that he was about to pass out. His eyes wouldn't open. His limbs wouldn't move. Time seemed to ebb and flow around him, as he fought to stay in control.

From outside the vehicle he thought he heard footsteps crunching in the snow. Or was he hallucinating?

"Move a muscle and I'll shoot you." It was Kodiak's voice, right in his ear. Cold fingers grabbed his face and held them in their viselike grip. "I will find Charlotte. You can't stop me."

A hard, sudden blow snapped Benjamin's head back against the seat.

Unconsciousness took hold.

FIFTEEN

A light flashed somewhere in the distance. Benjamin could hear a voice shouting, but far away, like someone trapped in the distant fog. His entire body ached and he could barely move. He forced his eyes open. He was in the upside-down, crushed hatchback—suspended by a seat belt with a face full of air bag. The beam of light scanned back and forth on the hill above him. A voice echoed, disjointed on the wind. "Hello? Hello? Is anyone there?"

"Over here!" He tried to shout but the words left his throat as barely more than a groan. He fumbled in the front pocket of his jeans for his pocketknife, yanked out the blade and hacked away at the seat belt. He fell free and crumbled into a ball on the ceiling of the car. The door was bent in and the handle wouldn't move, but he kicked the door hard with both feet, pounding into the metal until it flew open. He crawled out.

He was at the bottom of a steep hill. A wall of snow and trees rose above him. It was a wonder anyone had been able to find him down here.

"Benjamin!"

He blinked, unable to let his heart believe what his eyes were seeing.

Piper was running down the hill toward him.

Strength surged in his chest. He pulled himself to his feet. She flew into his arms and her lips brushed his cheek. "Benjamin! Are you okay? What happened? Where are you hurt?"

"Kodiak ran me off the road." And that was it. He suddenly lost the ability to find words to speak. One moment he'd thought he was about to die. The next, Piper was running down the snow toward him. He held her close. "Piper…" His hands cupped her face. "Is it really you?"

"Yeah." A laugh of relief slipped through her lips. "It's really me, I'm really here. But more importantly, how are you? What happened? Can you walk?"

His arms slid around her waist and pulled her tightly against him. Was she kidding? Just knowing he was still alive and she was here, he felt as if he could fly. "Yeah, I can walk. Everything aches, but I've been worse. Between the air bag, the seat belt, the deep snow and the layers of winter clothes I have on, I seemed to be pretty well cushioned." His lips brushed her cheeks and he tasted tears. So many questions were tumbling through his mind that he didn't know where to start. There were probably just as many tumbling through hers. "How did you find me?"

"When you didn't answer your phone, I called your sister." Piper had called Meg? But why? His head was still spinning and Piper was talking so fast she was barely pausing for breath. "She told me the route you were taking and told me where she'd lost your signal.

When I spotted the smashed railing I followed the footprints down and trail of debris and Dominic's things—"

"Dominic's things?" He pulled back and followed a few steps around the back of the car in the direction she was pointing. The back of the hatchback was smashed open. The contents of Dominic's boxes were strewn in the snow. "Kodiak must've come down the hill through the snow to steal something by the look of it. But what could he possibly be after in Dominic's stuff?"

"My guess? The newspaper star I made my aunt. Dominic's the guy Charlotte was sneaking out to see. Probably even the person Uncle Des saw her kissing. She apparently stole my newspaper star and gave it to him. Maybe that's even what Trisha had Gavin looking for when he trashed all the Christmas decorations in the barn. Alpha did text something about checking in 'Christmas things.'"

There were so many questions cascading through his mind he didn't even know where to start. "How would he find Charlotte from a newspaper star you made your aunt as a child?"

"No idea. Maybe Charlotte wrote something on it before she gave it to Dominic. Some sort of address, phone number or clue to where she is now. Then again, I made it out of very old newspapers I found in the basement and Charlotte was studying history. Maybe she thought it was worth something. Because Alpha was tracking her down, maybe she gave it to Dominic for safekeeping. We might never know." Her hand slid over his arm. "There's a whole lot we still need to talk about, but all that really matters right now is that it's cold, you just survived a car accident and we still have to get you to your sister's wedding. Come on. There's hot coffee and cookies in the truck. I called 911 before I walked down the hill, so police and ambulance are already on their way."

They climbed up the steep hill, walking slowly as Benjamin gingerly tested his limbs for injuries. The remnants of Dominic's boxes lay around them, slowly disappearing under a dusting of snow. The star was nowhere to be seen. They trudged upward. Something was niggling at the back of his mind, something very important about Christmas and Piper being here. But his head still ached and his mind was swimming in so many circles it was hard to focus.

His eyes rose to the highway above and he was so shocked by what he saw that he could barely believe he wasn't hallucinating. "Is that my truck?"

"Yes!" Happiness shone in Piper's eyes. "That's why I called your sister to begin with and then came after you. I managed to get it back for you, along with your bag, your passport, your ticket—everything. All of it. It's all right there. Now, you can catch your flight tomorrow."

For a moment he couldn't tell if she was laughing or crying. He grabbed her around the waist and hugged her so tightly her feet left the ground. Then they climbed into the truck. She pulled out a Thermos from behind the passenger seat.

"Like I said, we have a whole lot to talk about. Blondie in the navy ski mask was Trisha. She wore a wig and mask when she was stalking me and a fake belly when she wasn't. You were right when you said we should think about how clothes disguise people." She poured him a cup of coffee. The steam rose. "I caught her poking around the basement, chased her down and tackled her."

"Nice!" Again that unsettling feeling that he was forgetting to ask her about something important kicked at the back of his brain. He glanced at the clock. Quarter to twelve. He'd been out for over an hour.

"Thanks." Piper smiled. "I convinced her to tell me where she'd hidden your truck. She also backed up everything that Gavin said and most of what we suspected."

He raised the cup to his lips and drank. He'd never tasted better coffee. "She was working for Alpha?"

"Worse. She was dating Alpha. Exact same story, just six years later. They met online. He got scary. She wanted to get away from him. Only she says he started slipping sometimes and calling her 'Charlotte' when he was upset and demanding she wear a blond wig so she looked like her, too. Creepy stuff. She thought finding Charlotte for him would be her way out. When he told her that Charlotte said she'd be here this Christmas, she offered to come to The Downs and convince Charlotte to take him back. Took Gavin with her as backup, pretended to be sick and pregnant so Gavin would keep his distance, and created a cover story for them in case Charlotte needed convincing." She leveled her eyes at him over the mug. "I get the impression she was more than ready to kidnap Charlotte if that's what it took to get Alpha off her back. Only when she got here, she couldn't find Charlotte."

"Did she give you Alpha's name?"

"No, that's one thing she wouldn't spill. I get the impression she's really scared of him. It was like part of her was kind of relieved to be arrested. But she didn't deny it when I accused her of breaking into my room at night. Alpha apparently texted her that he'd actually seen Charlotte go into my room, so she was really surprised when she broke in and it was just me. The weirdest part of the whole thing for me is, just like Gavin said, Alpha's texts started getting bizarre until she had no idea what she was looking for or where."

Like "check the Christmas things" and "check the brick."

Flashing red-and-blue lights were coming toward them. "How did Kodiak know that I had the newspaper star? And even if Charlotte had written her address and phone number on the thing, why would Alpha think he could still use it to trace her six years later?"

A police car pulled in front of them. Another stopped behind.

"No idea," Piper said. She ran both hands through her hair. "Aunt Cass and Uncle Des are working out an arrangement with Dominic where he takes a suite whenever we have guests so I'm never staying there alone with strangers. And if I ever do manage a night without guests, I'll stay over at Silver Halls with Aunt Cass and Uncle Des. Now that Trisha and Gavin have been arrested, police are hopeful the harassment will stop. But they'll also be doing a media blitz about everything that's happened, which will hopefully get word back to Alpha that there's no point looking for Charlotte at The Downs. Oh, and they have a pretty good suspect on Kodiak, too. They think he might be a career criminal called Cody Aliston, so they're issuing a warrant. Hopefully, this will all be the end of it."

The end of it. So that was it? It was over? Benjamin ran both hands over his face feeling as if he'd been knocked out for months instead of minutes. It was like waking up from a coma to catch up on the story that had been his life. Only instead of having people urgently trying to tell him everything that had gone wrong in his absence, this time everything had been wrapped up. He'd missed the finale, and other people had stepped up to do what he hadn't been able to.

Piper didn't need him as her hero.

There was nothing to stop him from catching his Christmas flight.

"Christmas Eve at The Downs!" He grabbed her hand, as he suddenly realized what had been kicking the back of his brain. What was Piper doing here, sitting beside him in his truck, when she had a huge event to run? "You've got to get back to The Downs!"

"It's fine." She pulled her hand away from his. Cops were walking to her door. "Aunt Cass and Uncle Des have it covered. They're scaling things down to what they can manage and relying on a lot of volunteers. Someone needed to bring you your stuff and it made the most sense for it to be me. Not to mention your truck is so much better for this weather than the hatchback you were driving. I was going to try to meet up with you, switch vehicles and drive Dominic's car back."

He glanced toward the cliff where the hatchback lay crushed at the base.

"Don't worry," Piper said, following his gaze. "My aunt's friend on the island has a spare car she'll lend me to get home."

He felt as if he should be arguing, but wasn't sure quite what to say. She couldn't just show up, say she was skipping the event she'd been single-mindedly focused on and not give him a real explanation.

What happened when I was unconscious? What am I missing?

And why won't Piper meet my eye?

An officer knocked on the truck door.

"Christmas Eve happens every year. Your sister and her fiancé only get married once." She squeezed Benjamin's arm, but her gaze wouldn't quite meet his. "There isn't enough time to get me back to The Downs and you to the island both, and we can hardly expect the cops to ferry us around the province. Let's just hope we can file a report and get you checked out quickly, so you can still make it home for the wedding."

They drove to the island in uncomfortable silence, both of them staring straight ahead through the windshield at the lightly falling snow.

Piper glanced over at Benjamin as he slowed the truck to cross the swing bridge to Manitoulin Island. Thankfully, despite the fact Benjamin's jacket hid some impressively large bruises on his arms and chest, the paramedics had been convinced to let him continue on to Meg's wedding. The police had even given them an escort for a while, until the cruiser turned off to head back to the closest provincial division.

But the joy-filled thankfulness and relief that seemed to fill Benjamin when she'd first found him had descended into awkwardness. He wanted her to go back to The Downs. That much was clear. But there wasn't any time. Benjamin's large, sturdy four-wheel truck had the best possible chance of cutting it through the storm and getting him to the island on time. Dropping her off at a car-rental place at night on Christmas Eve was silly when there was a vehicle waiting on the island she could borrow.

But still they'd argued and when she hadn't given in, he'd lapsed into stony silence.

She'd made peace with her decision to miss Christmas Eve. Why couldn't he? As the truck mounted the bridge she looked down at the frozen lake spread out on either side, icy gray with dark waters showing here and there through the surface.

He didn't understand what had happened in those minutes between when he left and when she found him, and she'd never explain it to him.

Her uncle and aunt had taken her aside. Aunt Cass had held her hands when she had told her, *"Get in the truck, go after Benjamin. Make sure he gets his stuff on time and that he walks into his sister's wedding with none of that stress on his shoulders."*

"I'll miss Christmas Eve."

A soft light had twinkled in her aunt's eyes. *"But, you'll be giving someone you love both peace of mind and joy—which this Christmas might just be the best gift you can give him."*

Someone she loved? What did her aunt think she'd seen when she'd watched the two of them say goodbye?

"Trust me." Uncle Des's hand had fallen on her shoulder. "Your aunt and I have been managing bigger crises than this together long before you were born. We're built of stronger stuff than you seem to think sometimes. Benjamin's a good man and that's some talk he gives on chasing dreams and taking chances. So go. Wish him a merry Christmas from us and then come home in time for Christmas morning. We'll be okay."

So she'd followed Benjamin. She'd followed the route

he'd sent his sister, down snowy, twisting back roads in a storm. She'd done that one thing she promised herself she'd never do—left what mattered most to her and followed a man, because she realized she'd loved him.

Even though everything about him now seemed to indicate he wished she wasn't there.

Benjamin looked at the clock on the dashboard. It was five thirty. He frowned. "The church is still half an hour from here. We're not going to make it for the start of the service. I'm just going to skip it, go home, get changed and show up at the reception."

"You'll make it. It'll be tight but—"

"I'm wearing grease-stained jeans with giant holes in the knees. I'm a mess from the car crash. I have to get cleaned up and change into my tux. I need to shave and—"

"Your sister won't care about any of that!" Why was he even arguing about this? Her eyes scanned the torn jeans and plaid shirt that fit him as comfortably as a second skin. "Your sister loves *you*, more than anything! You can show up dressed just as you are and she won't care."

No response. Just a deeper frown. It was as if he wasn't even hearing her and instead just listening to a voice in his head that only he could hear—one that seemed to be berating him.

"It doesn't matter," he said. "It's too late, anyway. While you were talking to the police, I borrowed an officer's phone, called her and told her she'd have to go ahead and get married without me."

"But we're so close now!" Piper argued. "We can call her on my phone, tell her we're only thirty minutes out, and ask her to postpone the wedding for an hour. You know she will."

"But she shouldn't have to!" Benjamin smacked the steering wheel. His voice echoed through the cab. When he glanced at Piper her heart leaped in her chest. Behind the frustration burning like flames in the blue of his eyes echoed a deeper pain than she'd ever seen there before. "You don't get it, Piper. I've let my sister down. Again! And I made you miss your big important Christmas Eve thing."

But you don't understand! I chose to miss it. I chose you.

And I don't know how to tell you that.

She opened her mouth to speak, but he waved her down.

"Please, don't try to tell me it's not my fault, that it's because of Charlotte, or Gavin, or Trisha, or Kodiak, or Alpha. I made choices. Me. I chose not to lock my truck outside the barn when Trisha stole it. I chose not to shoot Trisha when she escaped through the snow and not to choke Kodiak until he was unconscious when I caught him in the alleyway. I chose to take an empty back highway to get to the island instead of inching along the main road. I..." He took a deep breath. Then his chest fell. "I chose to come see you and drop the dog off in person, because I wanted to see you one more time before I went. If I hadn't done that you might not have even been down by the barn for Kodiak to attack you."

But you saved me!

She waited a moment while he crossed the bridge. Then they hit shore.

"Everyone makes mistakes," she said softly.

"Yeah, but my mistakes hurt people, Piper. Don't

you get that?" The truck wound through the narrow, island highway. "My mistakes hurt people. I made the mistake of not wearing a helmet snowmobiling when I was fifteen years old, and my sister spent years paying for that. You know the accident happened just two weeks before her birthday? So instead of having a party and opening gifts, she spent the day huddled around my hospital bed, wondering if I was ever going to wake up from the coma."

She slid her hand across the seat toward him. He didn't take it.

"I made my sister miss her high school graduation, too," he added, "and her plans to go away for university, and my folks' plans to go to Florida for their thirty-fifth wedding anniversary. My sister couldn't go anywhere on the island, for the whole rest of her life, without people trying to talk to her about the most traumatic thing she'd ever lived through. No wonder she had anxiety. She lost so much all because I was the dummy who went snowmobiling without a helmet."

He ran his hands over his head. "So, I don't do that anymore. Got it? I'm not the guy who causes problems anymore. I'm the guy who fixes them. I'm the one who finds solutions and makes them happen. I'm not the problem that other people have to worry about. Not anymore. Not for Meg. Not..." His eyes glanced at her face for a moment before snapping back to the road. "Not...for anyone."

What was he saying? That he thought *he* was a problem for *her*?

He looked so pained and frustrated with himself.

She pulled her hand back and crossed her arms. "You're right. You went snowmobiling without a helmet, underage, on a highway, without a license, and got hit by a transport truck. You were badly hurt. You hurt people who loved you. Those were some colossally dumb decisions you made right there."

His eyebrow rose. "I can't believe you just said that."

"I'm not going to sugarcoat it," she said. "I don't think you'd want me to. But it's the decisions you made after that which matter. You decided to own up to what you'd done, and create an incredible sports business. You encouraged other people to take risks, be brave and live their life to the fullest while teaching them to also be smart and safe at the same time. That's pretty amazing. Now you're about to fly overseas and sail the world. You take more risks than anyone else I know."

Benjamin didn't meet her eye. "No, I don't," he said quietly. "Not where other people's hearts are concerned." He slowed at a traffic sign. "Oh, sure, I bungee jump and kayak and rappel. But that's just the science of levers and pulleys and helmets. Controllable, predictable elements. But other people's feelings..." His voice trailed off.

Shivers ran down Piper's arms and down her spine. She knew what he didn't say. Other people's feelings weren't always controllable or predictable.

He pulled through the intersection and kept driving. "Your uncle Des came out to say goodbye when I left. Thanked me for a talk of mine he'd heard. Said it really encouraged him to think through what risks he was willing to take in his future. Called me brave." He shrugged. "All I could think was that he was the brave one. Your uncle has been with the same woman for over forty years! They survived moving from one country to another, the bottom falling out of his work and not being able to move back. They went through not being able to have kids of their own. They took you in and raised you. Now they're facing years of health problems."

The truck left the small town and pulled onto another rural road.

"Your uncle is a braver man than I will ever be. I've been responsible for only one person my whole life, my sister. But I always had total faith that was temporary, and one day she'd be standing on her own two feet. That was it. That was my one shot being somebody else's guardian. I can't ever be anyone's full-time, solid rock and anchor person. Not like your uncle and aunt are for each other. Because if I did and I let that person down, I'd never forgive myself. That's what I was trying to tell you back in the restaurant on the island last summer, when you suddenly had to get up and go. I just can't ever let myself—"

A car whipped around them and Benjamin hit the brakes in a controlled skid.

His hand landed hard on the horn.

Finish the sentence, she wanted to yell at him. *You can't let yourself what?*

But he obviously wasn't ready to finish his thought and she wasn't about to push. She pressed her lips together and forced herself to wait. The sign for his town loomed ahead of them.

"Meg asked me to walk her down the aisle," he said after a few long minutes. "Now, she's the kind of independent woman who'd be quite happy walking herself down the aisle. But she asked me. And…and everybody in that church is going to look at me and still think of me as that irresponsible younger brother who wrecked the family's life, no matter how hard I worked to fix what I'd done. They're all going to see me run in late, making her wait, in torn, stained jeans, and roll their eyes at how foolish, irresponsible Benji Duff is same as he ever was.

"I'm going to ruin her special moment!" His voice rose. "It was always going to be like that. Even if there was some way I could rush home, shave, cut my hair, put on a tux and show up looking like a million bucks, what difference would it make, really? They're all going to know that I'm not good enough for that honor! I'll know that I'm not good enough."

And there it was.

"So, don't be good enough." Her hand slipped onto his arm. "Whatever being 'good enough' is even supposed to mean. She didn't ask you to be good enough. She asked you to be there. So, go. Go be your sister's guardian and best friend one last time. She's strong enough to tell you to go home and change, and delay things while you do. Just show up, right now, in your old jeans and red plaid shirt, and be her brother. Not because you're perfect, worthy, or what somebody else might say is 'good enough.' But because you're the only sibling each other has got and you love each other, and that's all that actually matters."

He blew out a long breath. She closed her eyes, leaned her head back against the seat and let her heart pray with feelings she didn't even know how to put into words.

The truck stopped and she opened her eyes. A small country church sat ahead of them. The clock read six fourteen.

Benjamin unbuckled his seat belt. "Come on. If I'm doing this thing you're coming in with me."

He leaped from the truck and ran through the snow toward the small church. Piper followed. His footsteps pounded up the church steps and he opened the door. There stood Meg, beautiful and breathtaking in a dazzling white beaded dress, trimmed with a white cloak lined with deep red velvet.

Tears slipped from the bride's eyes. "You made it!"

Benjamin swallowed hard. "Of course."

Piper stepped back. But Meg's joy-filled eyes swept over her, her gaze pulling her in. "Thank you so much for bringing my brother to me. Please stay. I'd be so happy to have you. You're welcome just the way you are, but if you want something fancier for the reception, one of my friends runs a consignment formal-wear shop. I'm sure she will be more than happy to help you pop out and find something to wear right after the service." Then Meg squeezed her brother's arm, pulling him to her. "Come on, baby bro. Let's go do this."

Piper waited until the bride and her brother started down the aisle toward her groom. Then she slipped in the back of the church and found space at the end of a pew.

The service was beautiful. She'd never seen two people more excited to start a life together. Carols were sung, candles lit, vows exchanged. Jack's best man, Luke, and his fiancée, Nicky, stood up to read the beautiful familiar Old Testament reading. "Many waters cannot quench love. Rivers cannot sweep it away."

Yet somehow, through it all, she only had eyes for the scruffy, beaming, jean-clad Benjamin. Her heart sobbed.

Her uncle and aunt were right, as much as she didn't want to admit it to herself and would never admit it to

Benjamin. She loved him. She'd cared for him since the first moment she'd laid eyes on him last summer, and the feeling had grown inside her until she ached just to be near him. She loved him so much she wanted him to get on that plane tomorrow, fly to Australia, sail the world and make every one of his dreams come true.

She loved him so much she wanted him to leave.

Lord, why is it the only man I could ever imagine going through this life with is the one so determined to never share his life with anyone?

Was she so much like her mother that she was only attracted to men who were destined to leave? At least Benjamin had always been honest with her.

The congregation stood to sing "Joy to The World" as the wedding party started back down the aisle. Piper got up from her seat and slipped out the door.

She couldn't do this. She couldn't stay. She couldn't get dressed up and go to the reception and hang on to Benjamin's arm as if she belonged there, only to watch him leave again.

Lord, give me the strength to say goodbye to this dream.

She walked through town, her boots crunching through the snow as the dark night settled in around her. She reached her aunt's friend who'd offered her a car. After a quick hug and thank-you, Piper was back on the road, driving back over the bridge, toward home. Her phone started ringing. She glanced down. It was Benjamin. She ignored it, even when it rang again. She didn't pick up but instead texted back a quick line to tell him to thank Meg for the invite but that she was heading home.

Then she turned her phone off.

* * *

Benjamin frowned at his phone and then set it down on the table. Piper wasn't answering. The flurry of well-wishers who'd come by the head table to ask about his sailing trip had finally trickled off. He'd heard every conceivable joke about showing up at his sister's wedding dressed as a lumberjack. But Meg was happy. The moment he'd seen that joy light up in her eyes he'd known he'd made the right decision.

He looked down at the wedding cake in front of him. Considering how many years Meg had run the top wedding planning business on the island, it was no wonder the food was impeccable. But somehow, every bite had seemed to land in his stomach like sawdust.

Meg swirled off her happy husband's arm and spun across the floor toward Benjamin. She dropped into a chair beside him and squeezed his arm, her face flushed with both excitement and fatigue. "Did you ever manage to get through to Piper?"

"No." Somehow he'd lost sight of her in the hustle of the wedding, but had tried calling to give her the location of the reception. She'd have known the restaurant, since it was where they'd had their last meal together before she'd left the island last summer. In fact, the door she walked out of was right over there. "She isn't answering her phone, but she did send a text message saying she'd decided to go back home."

"Oh?" Meg said. It was amazing how much inflection his sister was able to put in one syllable.

Suddenly, he felt himself blushing. "Yeah, well, the drive here was a bit tense. I told her to head back to The Downs. Maybe she thought I didn't want her here."

Meg's eyebrow rose.

"But it wasn't that," he said quickly. "It was more that I didn't want her to go to any trouble for me or give up on anything that mattered. I tried to explain that I never wanted to be responsible for anyone else's happiness, because I can't trust that I'd never let them down or hurt them."

He slid his head into his hands. It had almost felt as if they were arguing. But he wasn't quite sure what about. Being run off the road like that had reminded him of just how determined he was to never make a commitment to someone else that he might not be able to keep. She hadn't even disagreed with him on any of that.

Meg pulled her chair back against the wall and gestured to him to follow. He did so.

"Two of the people who were stalking The Downs have been arrested," he added. "She's going to have a friend stay there whenever she has guests so she won't be alone with strangers. She tried to make it sound like all the problems of the last few days are sorted and there's nothing else I can do. And she's right, there's not really anything much I can do. So, I don't understand why I'm beating myself up for letting her leave and why my insides feel like they're being mangled in a car crusher."

"You are unbelievable." Meg crossed her arms. Her smile was somewhere between frustrated and amused. "For a long time I thought you were the smartest guy I knew, and now I've never heard you sound so clueless. You're in love with this woman, Benjamin. I saw it in your eyes the first time you mentioned her name, and here she loves you well enough to skip the biggest night of her year and drive fourteen hours round-trip just to make sure you had your passport."

Benjamin could feel a flush rising to his cheeks. "You don't get it, Meg. Even if I did have feelings for Piper, there's nothing I can do about it. I'm sitting at my sister's wedding. I'm flying to Australia tomorrow night. I have a boat, a sailing trip and a new life waiting for me on the other side of the world. She's committed to spending the rest of her life taking care of her uncle and aunt, running a bed-and-breakfast in a town even smaller than this one. She's not happy there and I for sure wouldn't be. Look, it doesn't matter how I *feel*. There's absolutely nothing I can *do*."

His words spluttered to a stop like an engine that had just run out of steam.

Meg nodded. She leaned forward, gathering her billowing dress around her just like she used to do when she was playing dress-up as a child. "Remember that game we used to play as kids where one of us asks a question and the other has to answer it as fast as they can with the first thing that pops into their mind?"

"Yeah?"

"Where do you want to spend Christmas?"

"With Piper." The answer flew from his heart to his lips without a second's hesitation.

"Then what are you doing here? Get yourself back in your truck and go spend Christmas with her."

"But that's a seven-hour drive!"

"I know."

"And I'm flying to Australia tomorrow night."

"Yup. Good thing your bag is all packed and The Downs is only a couple of hours from the Toronto airport." She was smiling now. It was infuriating.

"Meg! I'm at *your* wedding reception!"

"Yes, and you've walked with me down the aisle, I've

gotten married, the pictures have been taken and the cake's been cut." She grabbed his arm and yanked him out of the chair. "We can open presents without you."

He was already climbing to his feet. "But I don't know what I'm going to say to Piper. I don't know how to explain why I'm back. I don't even know what I want to do. She still can't come to Australia and I still don't want to stay at The Downs."

"It's okay." She stood, too, and slipped her arms around her brother. "You've always been good at figuring out what to do on the fly. Just pretend you're sky-diving, or bungee jumping, or some other crazy, risky thing you went and did that scared the life out of you right before you leaped. Now go, before anyone tries to stop you and talk. I'll say goodbye for you." When he hesitated, she pushed him hard with both hands. "Go!"

He got in the truck and drove through the night. Crisscrossing the province on Christmas Eve probably wasn't the wisest, most well-thought-out decision he'd ever made. But for the first time since Piper had walked out of that restaurant back on the island, he felt as if he was doing exactly what his heart wanted to, and as if every part of his body, heart and mind were finally playing on the same team.

No matter what happened next, it was a wonderful feeling.

It was almost four thirty when he pulled into The Downs parking lot. The lights were still out. Not even a twinkle of Christmas lights in the window or the gentle glow from an upstairs room. He got out of the truck and walked across the snow. Three sets of footprints lay in the snow in front of him. Piper, Dominic and...somebody else? He pulled the hidden key from under a rock by the door, but when he tried it, the front door wouldn't open. The garage door wouldn't open, either. He rounded the back of the house. The back door wouldn't even budge. His eyes scanned the darkened house.

Okay, now what?

He hadn't thought through how he was going to get in the house and didn't want to bang so hard he woke Piper up. But a window on the second floor was open. Well, looked as if his options now were climbing the fire escape and shimmying through a window or sleeping in his truck.

Then he heard the sound of crying. The sad, high-pitched sound floated on the winter air. He followed the sound. It was coming from the wooden kindling box beside the woodpile.

He ran toward the sound. "It's okay. I'm coming."

The whimpering grew louder. He pulled back the latch and threw the lid open. A ball of black-and-white fur launched himself into Benjamin's arms.

"Hey!" Benjamin cradled the dog in his arms and set him gently in the snow. "Are you okay? Did someone hurt you?"

Harry galloped out into the snow a few feet and then back again. Benjamin crouched and ran his hands through the dog's fur checking for injuries. It smelled sickly sweet.

Like chloroform.

A loud boom sounded below him, as if someone was shaking the very foundations of The Downs. A dim light flickered in the basement window. He crouched and looked in.

A figure was standing in the basement, swinging a

sledgehammer, knocking blow after blow hard into The Downs's foundation. Benjamin couldn't see his face.

The man disappeared from view and what he saw next made Benjamin gasp.

Piper was sitting in front of a small folding table. Her head drooped against her chest. Her hands were tied behind her to opposite legs of her chair.

The newspaper star was spread out in pieces on the table in front of her.

SIXTEEN

Piper's mind swam slowly up into consciousness, as disjointed thoughts and feelings filled her senses. She felt rope dig sharply into her wrists, saw scraps of newspaper float on the table in front of her like scattered islands of letters and shapes. A flashlight lay nearby sending a triangle of yellow light across the table and over the floor. A loud, constant thumping split the air, shattering the concrete walls, exposing the bare brick beneath. The sound seemed to rattle her eardrums and shatter the inside of her skull.

It was as if someone was trying to bring The Downs crashing down with her inside it.

Her eyes fluttered shut again, as memories assailed her.

It had been quarter after three when she'd gotten home. The Downs had seemed eerily empty. No Dominic. No dog. Yet candles had flickered in the living room, covering every possible surface of the room like someone's creepy idea of a romance.

Then a hand had grabbed her neck, and a gun barrel had pressed against her temple. A cloth had been clamped over her face filling her nose with the smell of something sickly sweet.

Now she gasped in a deep breath, filled her lungs and screamed.

"Piper!" The thumping stopped and a man ran out of the darkness toward her. "Don't scream. It's all going to be okay. Just do what I say, and then I can let you go."

Slowly her eyes rose toward him. His hand clenched a sledgehammer. Brick dust covered his body. His face was half-hidden in shadows, but she saw enough to gasp in horror.

"Dominic?"

No. It couldn't be. The young man she'd known since they were kids, who loved his huge family of nieces and nephews and was training to be a cop—*he* was the man now standing over her as she was tied, helpless, to this chair?

"Let me go. Please, Dominic. I don't know what's going on here or what you think you're doing but you have to let me go."

He broke her gaze and gestured toward the scraps of paper on the table in front of her. "Figure out what that means, then this'll all be over."

He raised the sledgehammer high, turned back to the wall and swung. She didn't even glance down at the paper he pointed to.

"I don't care about some paper star or where Charlotte is now!" Her voice was swallowed up by the deafening blows landing against the brick in the darkness. "I care about the fact my friend attacked me and tied me to a chair. What happened to you? What happened to the Dominic I know? Remember when we were seven and I climbed that tree in the park to get your kite back?

Or when we were ten and your family went on holiday so you asked me to come over every day to feed your turtle? Please! Dominic, you're scaring me!"

The thumping stopped. Dominic turned. His face was so pale in the lamplight it was almost white. His eyes darted past her into the darkness.

"It's okay, Piper. I don't want to hurt you. Just focus on solving the puzzle, and it'll be all over soon enough. Please."

The puzzle? She stared down at the table. Someone had taken apart the Christmas star she'd made as a child and spread the pieces over the table, pushing the pieces together at the corners and lining up the lines as best they could. It was a page of newsprint, with headlines about Christmas holidays and fairs, just like a regular community paper.

The date at the top read *December 25, 1924.*

It was issued during American Prohibition, and when Canada's alcohol was under tight government control.

Right around the time of The Downs's rumored speakeasy and smuggling past.

"What are you doing?" she asked him. "What do you think is behind those walls?"

He didn't respond.

Years ago Charlotte had come here looking for a speakeasy. She'd always told Piper so.

And I hadn't believed her, because I'd stopped believing it was real.

But Charlotte had believed. She'd fallen hook, line and sinker for the tales of walls stacked with old, frosted glass bottles of bootleg rum, hidden envelopes of money, bags of jewelry and loot from ill-gotten gains. Charlotte hadn't just robbed The Downs. She'd searched it for some hidden treasure she could use to get away from Alpha.

What if she'd found it?

Piper stared back at the paper. Some lines were darker than others, just slightly, as if the printing plates had been uneven with ink. Subtly, in ways she'd never noticed as a child. Now her adult eyes traced and connected the darker letters like a grid. It looked like there were *blueprints* hidden within the words on the page. If she joined up the vertical and horizontal lines the pattern they formed created walls, entrances, and hallways. But pieces of the page were missing. Strips here. Jagged pieces there. Holes from where she'd torn the paper in her youthful enthusiasm.

"This isn't the whole page," she said. "There are pieces missing."

"Just focus on remembering." Dominic shifted his weight and started on another wall. "Keep reading and fill in the blanks."

So he didn't know about the blueprints and thought it was nothing more than newspaper articles. He might have no clue why Charlotte had stolen this star or what it had to do with finding her. Dominic's swings grew faster, harder. At this rate he'd bring the entire house down.

"But I was a child when made this. I have no way of knowing what was here."

"Piper, please!" Dominic's voice rose, filling the basement. "All we have to do is find Charlotte and then this will all be over."

Find Charlotte? Charlotte was a person. Not a hundred-year-old rumor from history, an object hidden in a box of

Christmas decorations or something to find by bashing holes in a wall. Had Dominic lost his mind?

The longer she stared at the paper the clearer the hidden blueprints were appearing. Tunnels were appearing on the page now, a passageway, and what looked like a hidden room.

"Untie my hands. Please." She kept her voice level and firm, pushing through the fear even as it threatened to take her over.

"I'm sorry. I'm so sorry, Pips. I would if I could, but I can't."

Again, Dominic's eyes flitted to the shadows and then around the room, like a mosquito trapped in a jar. Her head turned. But all she could see was the darkness looming in from the corners of the room and filling the cluttered basement.

"Why? Why can't you, Dominic?"

No answer. Sweat ran down Dominic's face. Was he frightened, paranoid, on drugs?

"Dominic! Talk to me! This is crazy. Whatever's going on, I can help you!"

"Just find Charlotte, Pips. Please."

He stepped out of the light and into the darkness. She watched his shadow on the floor as he swung a sledgehammer high over his head. The banging started up again.

Oh, Lord, help me please.

She lowered her head as fear and frustration battled in her mind, laced with a toxic confusion that threatened her ability to even think straight. Her vision swam before her, the pieces fading in and out of focus. They were definitely blueprints, a map. But not for the basement Dominic was desperately chipping away at piece by piece. Nor the barn that Gavin had demolished.

These were blueprints for the main floor of The Downs.

There was the staircase. Here was the entrance to the basement. There was the fireplace—

Something about Christmas things...

Something about brick...

Then suddenly, her gut told her all too well what Charlotte had discovered and why she'd demolished the Christmas tree and decorations to find it. Even why someone would come back here looking for her now— the final winter before they were due to break ground for The Downs renovations.

"I think I know where Charlotte went!"

Dominic froze. Something rustled behind her in the darkness.

"But I won't know for sure without my hands. Some of these pieces aren't in the right place."

Dominic nodded. "Okay. But just one hand."

One hand would have to do.

"Okay. Just one. That's all I need."

Dominic stepped closer. Then he bent down and touched her left hand. His voice dropped until it was barely a whisper. "You know I care about you, Pip, right?"

She nodded to show she'd heard him. But she didn't trust herself to respond.

"Forgive me, Pip." He untied the rope. Her left hand fell free.

"I forgive you, Dominic."

She gripped the chair with her right hand and leaped up, swinging the chair around above her head. It hit

Dominic hard on the side of the head, knocking him to the ground.

She scrambled across the floor, yanked her other hand free and grabbed the sledgehammer from the floor.

"Piper! Wait! Please!" Dominic's voice echoed up the stairs behind her. "You don't understand."

Oh, she understood well enough. She had to get upstairs. She had to call the cops.

She had to find Charlotte.

Her feet pounded up the stairs. Just three more steps and she'd be at the top.

A gunshot sounded behind her.

Dominic yelped.

His desperate scream was filled with such pain, it sent shivers through her body.

Then his voice fell silent.

She turned back. Dominic was lying on the floor in the basement now. Blood pooled beneath him.

A figure stood over him, his face hidden in the shadows.

"Hello, darling." A cold voice rasped from the darkness. "You really shouldn't have hit your friend like that. He was only trying to save you and his family. Wouldn't want all those precious little nieces and nephews to have something terrible happen to them on Christmas Day." Dark chuckles poured like ice water over her skin. "I told him I'd let you all live if he followed my instructions and did what I say. Not that I was ever going to let him go alive. Not after what he did."

The sledgehammer tightened in her grasp. She took a step backward up another step. Candlelight was flicking in the living room. Dim and faint. "You're Alpha?" Her feet were now just two steps from the top. "You were the cruel, mean, controlling boyfriend that both Charlotte and Trisha wanted so desperately to get away from. You terrified Charlotte, so much that she wouldn't even go to the cops. She had no family and you were paying her rent and tuition. She thought she could steal something valuable enough to gain her freedom or buy her way to a new life. But you wouldn't let her go, would you? You followed her here. You spied on her and Dominic."

"Stop it!" he bellowed up the stairs toward her. "He has no right to try to take my love from me!"

"But Charlotte got away, didn't she?" Her feet slid back up another step.

A floorboard creaked in the darkness behind her. Someone else was there in The Downs, behind her in the darkness.

Lord, as much as I wish Benjamin was here, I also hope he's still far, far away and in safety.

"Stop right there. Or I will hurt you." Alpha stepped forward slowly into the light. She saw two well-polished shoes. Tailored tweed pants. A cane.

Piper's free hand rose to her lips. *Tobias.*

The arrogant, delusional man who wrote books about warfare and torture, who in one moment would spout random things out of context and had confused both Trisha and Piper with university students, but in another was lucid enough to spin long, creative stories. He now stood in the tiny pocket of light at the bottom of the basement stairs, a gun in his outstretched hand, still smoking from shooting Dominic.

Ever since Kodiak had first attacked her by the barn it had almost felt like she was stuck in a time loop. Charlotte had come to The Downs six years ago. Yet, Alpha seemed to think she was there now.

What if, in Alpha's mind, it was still six years ago?

All this time she'd foolishly presumed Alpha had to be some young heartthrob to hold such sway over both Charlotte and Trisha. And not just because she'd thought Alpha, not Dominic, was the man Uncle Des had seen Charlotte kissing in the woods six years ago. *It's all about thinking like a predator, Piper.* Now she could imagine how a well-spoken, well-connected man might have sounded as the online suitor and financial benefactor to a vulnerable young woman so many years his junior.

"Surprised I see." A self-satisfied smirk curled at his lips, like a magician too proud of a conjuring trick. A chuckle rumbled in the back of his throat. "Oh, you'll be amazed what you can get a person to do for you if only you know how to motivate them properly. Charlotte and Trisha were all alone in the world and needed caring for. But a disappointing number of people are easy to control by nothing but a very generous check."

Through the blood pounding in her head she heard another footstep behind her. Someone was waiting behind her, hiding, and all she could hear was the sound of their breath.

Benjamin, I have no reason to believe you'd be here. But if you are, signal me somehow. Tell me what I can do to help you save us both.

Her voice rose. "But you failed, didn't you? Charlotte ran into the arms of another man. She came up with a plan to get away from you. Did you catch up with her before or after she destroyed my living room looking for the speakeasy?"

His smirk turned to a grimace.

"Let me guess," she said. "You found her and hurt

her, but she got away and you lost her in the house. You tore up The Downs looking for her, but she was gone."

If what Piper had guessed from reading those hidden blueprints was true, she could even forgive Charlotte for tearing down the tree and destroying the nativity. Pain and fear made people do desperate things.

Her hands tightened on the sledgehammer. She picked it up like a baseball bat. He might still have a gun pointed at her face, but just one good swing was all she'd need and then he'd be down. She backed up onto the last step, reaching the main floor. A hand brushed against her back in the darkness.

Benjamin?

Then a hand clamped her throat from behind, choking the air from her lungs. The other grabbed the sledgehammer and yanked her arm hard behind her back. Her wide eyes stared in horror at the crude bear tattoo on his wrist.

No. Benjamin was hours away celebrating happily with friends and family.

It was Kodiak.

Tobias laughed as Kodiak slowly wrenched her arm harder and harder until the sledgehammer fell with a reverberating thud.

Lord, don't let them get away with this. No matter what happens to me, may this monster get caught before he hurts one more woman.

She shook her head, forcing words out as the fingers on her throat slowly grew tighter. "I'm not one of those vulnerable women you can control, manipulate and scare into silence."

"Oh, but, Charlotte, you are." Tobias stepped closer, one step at a time, with an exaggerated, dramatic flair,

But her eyes shot upward toward the balcony. Was she praying? Did she know he was there?

"Don't you remember?" Tobias's voice echoed through the darkness. "I'm quite the expert in knowing how to hurt a woman so she isn't anywhere near dead, but wishes that she was. Apparently I was all too kind to you."

Then he strode into the living room and spread his arms like a maestro conducting a hidden symphony. Kodiak wrenched Piper's head back and forth so her gaze followed his employer's movements.

"From now on, you do not speak unless I direct you to." His voice rose as if he was addressing a full lecture hall. "Nod, Charlotte, to show you heard me."

She didn't move. Tobias snapped his fingers. Piper gritted her teeth as Kodiak forced her head up and down in a nodding motion.

"Oh, you think you're so strong, don't you?" Tobias's eyes grew cold. He nodded to Kodiak. "Break her arm."

Benjamin couldn't wait one second more. He leaped. His feet hit the back of an armchair just long enough to break his fall, before throwing himself at Kodiak. Out of the corner of his eye he could see Piper slam her elbow back into Kodiak's face and scramble from his grasp.

Kodiak swore in pain and lunged after her. But Benjamin got to him first. His fist flew, catching Kodiak in the jaw and sending him sprawling backward onto the floor. The vicious thug-for-hire leaped to his feet. A knife flashed in his hand. He lunged at Benjamin, with the glint in his eye of a man prepared to kill. Benjamin raised his arm and blocked the blow with one strong movement. Then he forced the attacker's arm down with so much speed that Kodiak's weapon landed deep in his own leg. Kodiak grunted, falling on his injured leg.

"Enough!" Tobias shouted. "Stop right this second! Nobody fights without my permission."

Yeah, that wasn't about to work on Kodiak right now, Benjamin thought, no matter how much Tobias was paying him.

From the corner of his eye, Benjamin saw Kodiak vault at him, landing on top of him. He grabbed Benjamin by the throat and began to squeeze. For a moment he could feel unconsciousness begin to overtake his mind. But this time he wasn't about to go under. He leveled a swift, decisive blow to Kodiak's jaw, followed by a second one that knocked the thug unconscious.

Benjamin climbed to his feet. One down.

Just a delusional madman to go.

"I said stop! Hands up. Or she will die!"

He turned. Tobias had Piper by the hair. Her dark mane was wrapped around one fist, while the other pressed a gun between her eyes.

"Hands up! Now! You think you can take Charlotte away from me?" Tobias's eyes bulged as he nudged Piper's face with the gun. Compliant, Benjamin lifted his hands. The man had completely lost his mind. "Charlotte is mine. Forever. Aren't you, Charlotte? You think she'd ever want a stupid, uneducated thug like you when she could have a real man taking care of her? A man like me?"

Piper's eyes met Benjamin's for one agonizing second. A prayer whispered across her lips. Then her eyes turned to her captor. She met his gaze without flinching.

"You found her here six years ago and you hurt her, didn't you?" Piper said. "Then you went home and got on with your life, finding and hurting other women, all while the memory of what you'd done to her haunted the edges of your rapidly failing mind. But when you saw in the paper that The Downs was about to be renovated, at least part of you worried your dirty little secret might come to light. So, you manipulated people into finding out what had happened to Charlotte. How frightened you must have been. Knowing your mind was slipping. Knowing you couldn't quite remember." She leaned closer, ignoring the gun, until her face was inches from his. "Having fleeting, painful, panicked moments, remembering just what you'd done to the woman you claimed to love, having them bashing up brick and tearing up rooms looking for her. Her dead body."

"Liar!" Tobias's outstretched hand flew toward her face. But she was too quick. Taking advantage of the momentary distraction, Piper broke free. She ducked under his arm and ran for the corner of the room.

That was the moment Benjamin was waiting for. He leaped forward, like a professional tackle. Tobias's weapon fired, seconds before it flew from his hands and clattered into the darkness. Benjamin knocked the would-be alpha to the ground.

But the cry of pain that echoed behind him filled his heart with the sinking knowledge he'd been too late.

The bullet had found its mark.

Piper had been shot.

He turned. "Piper!"

She was down on the ground, pulling herself toward the fireplace. Blood seeped from her pant leg.

"Go!" She grabbed the Christmas tree he'd made for her and used it to pull herself to her feet. "Take care of him. It's just a graze. I'll be okay."

"You really think you can escape and outsmart me this time?" Tobias crawled over to the table. "You think I wasn't prepared? I tried to warn you. I'm the master of booby traps and snares. I've locked all the doors, Charlotte. I've destroyed the stairs. I've hidden explosives at the exits and wired the windows so if you try to escape you'll die."

His eyes were wild, his gestures manic. He wiped blood from his face, then swept a candle up off the table and waved it over the woodpile that once was the stairs. Then he dropped it in.

"You think I just broke your generator to keep you in the dark? I wanted the fuel to start a fire to smoke you out if you didn't come to me. You can fight me until your energy fails. But trust me, there is no exit I haven't thought of and no contingency I haven't planned for."

But you never planned to face a man like me.

And Piper's no Charlotte.

Smoke billowed and flames flickered from the woodpile that had once been the stairs.

Benjamin spun toward Piper. She'd snapped off a hockey stick from the makeshift tree and slid it under her elbow as a crutch. She hobbled toward the fireplace.

"Find a way out!" Benjamin called. "Whatever it takes. Don't wait for me."

"You aren't going anywhere!" Blood poured from Tobias's chin. He pulled the small World War I grenade from his belt loop and waved it like a bone in front of a dog. "A warrior is always willing to die in battle and I will fight you with my dying breath."

Benjamin looked around. Fire rose from the pile of broken stairs. Flames raced up the long, lacy curtains and spread along the second-story balcony. Had Tobias really barricaded all the exits? Were there really booby traps and explosives? Could he risk it?

"Tobias, tell me how we get out of here! None of us needs to die here."

"He's a coward!" Piper shouted. "I suspect that grenade isn't even real. Even if it is, he doesn't have the courage to throw it!"

Benjamin had also presumed it was fake when he'd seen Tobias with it at breakfast yesterday. But what on earth was she doing, taunting a madman who might be holding something explosive?

"Go on!" Piper banged the end of her hockey stick on the floor. "If you think I'm Charlotte and you really want to prove I should fear you, throw it at me!"

Tobias snarled, pulled the pin and lobbed the grenade. Piper caught it in the air with the hockey stick, slapped it to the ground and sent it spinning into the fireplace.

Benjamin threw himself behind the sofa as he heard Piper call out his name.

Her next words were cut off in a rush of falling debris and a scream that seemed to echo from all directions.

A gaping hole in the floor now lay where the fireplace had been.

Piper was gone.

EIGHTEEN

"Piper!" Benjamin ran for the hole that was once a fireplace. He looked down into the darkness. "Are you all right?"

"I'm okay. I just lost my balance." Piper's voice floated up from the hole in the floor. "There seems to be a room down here. But I can't get back up. It must be a fifteen-foot drop."

"Stand back. I'm coming to get you."

Tobias was half sitting and half lying beside the table. Flames climbed the curtains behind him and smoke billowed around him. The second-story balcony was now alight. Tobias pulled a tiny pistol from his ankle and struggled to load it with bullets. "We will fight to the death, you and I. It will be a warrior's death and an honorable end to my life."

Benjamin shook his head in disgust. "There is no honor in murder. You can die if you want to die. I'd rather live."

He grabbed the remains of the Christmas tree, clipped the windup flashlight to his belt and wound the string of lights around his hand as a makeshift rappel rope to slow his decent.

He slid backward into the hole.

Darkness filled his eyes. Cold damp air seemed to press up against him. His feet hit cold stone and he struggled to maintain his balance. Then soft hands slid over his chest.

"Benjamin."

He felt Piper before he saw her. Her face pressed against his chest, then he lifted her head and his lips found hers in a kiss.

He slid one arm around her waist and felt her weight fall into his arms. "Are you hurt?"

"A bit. But I'm okay."

The flashlight whirred to life in his hands. They were standing in a wide cellar. Dusty bottles of amber liquid filled racks by the wall. The remains of a body lay on a bench by the wall, clad in a university jacket and sweatshirt.

Charlotte.

"Charlotte found the speakeasy, and we found her." A choke caught in Piper's throat. Benjamin's arm tightened around her waist and held her close to him. "She must have been so desperate to get away from him she was willing to rob me if that's what it took."

In her mind she created the scenario Charlotte must have faced years ago. "Tobias tracked her to The Downs and attacked her. She crawled in here hoping to hide and escape. She might have even been hoping that Dominic would decipher the star and find her. She probably didn't realize her wounds were fatal until it was too late. I think Tobias suspected she'd found the speakeasy and died here, but didn't know how to find it himself. Then when he read that we were planning to renovate the bed-and-breakfast, he panicked and realized her body might still be found, and there might be evidence on her that would point back to him." She shivered. "Maybe there still is."

She sat back against the crumbling wall. Gently, Benjamin used his knife to slit the bottom of her jeans from heel to calf. Then he tore a strip off the bottom of his sweatshirt and used it to bind Piper's leg wound. Thankfully, it looked as if the bullet had merely grazed her. "Can you walk?"

"Yeah. I think so."

But still, as he helped her to her feet, the wince that escaped from her lips and how deeply she leaned into his shoulder told him that it hurt her to stand. Burning and broken floorboards tumbled through the hole behind them bringing the fire with it. It probably wouldn't be too long before the entire floor above collapsed in. There was a lot of wood down here, not to mention flammable liquid.

He scanned the darkness for a way out and found a small opening on the far side of the room. It looked like a tunnel.

"Come on." He strengthened his grasp on her shoulders. "We've got to get out of here."

Her eyes met his. "Where's Harry?"

"He'll be okay. I left him in my truck with plenty of blankets and the door open, so he can jump out if he needed to. But The Downs is on fire. Once the flames reach down here, with all these bottles of bootleg liquor, the place will explode."

Her arm slid around Benjamin's waist. They ran.

The tunnel was dark and sloped downhill so steeply they could barely see. Walls pressed in on every side. The smell of smoke chased after them. Then they could hear the pop of bottles exploding as the fire reached the speakeasy. They kept running, until the ground sloped down so steeply they lost their footing and went into a slide.

Right into a solid brick wall.

They were trapped.

Panic thudded in Piper's chest.

The air wouldn't last forever and there was no way back. No, they couldn't die trapped here in the ground like this.

Help us, Lord. Show us the way out.

Benjamin shone the windup light in all directions. Above them he saw a shaft. He pressed the flashlight into her hands. "I'm going to try climbing. You going to be okay?"

She nodded and leaned against the hockey-stick crutch. "Yeah, go ahead."

He started climbing, finding holes and ledges for his fingers and toes in the brick. Then he stopped. "There are some loose bricks up here. But I need something to dig them out with."

She braced herself against the wall and passed up the hockey stick. "Here, use this. It's not going to be much use to me if we can't get out of here."

She waited, breathing through the pain, as he started digging at the bricks with a piece of broken hockey stick. Then a dim light shone through the cracks.

"Thank You, God!" Benjamin shouted an echo of the prayer filling her heart.

The hole grew larger. Then soft white snow fell in toward them.

"Where are we?" she called.

"The barn. I'm pretty glad I smashed my truck into your chimney now. I think I might have busted us an exit."

He hopped down, grabbed Piper around the waist and gently lifted her up until she could crawl out into the snow. Then he crawled through after her and stood. They were beside the remains of the barn, back where Benjamin had saved her from Kodiak two days ago.

The sun was beginning to rise over the tops of the trees.

It was Christmas morning.

Benjamin lifted her up off the ground and into the shelter of his arms.

She slid her arms inside his coat and felt the warmth of his chest. "Thank you for coming back for me."

"There's nowhere else I'd rather be." The scruff of his cheek brushed her face. Then she felt his lips on hers, kissing her deeply.

Smoke billowed through the snow above them. Emergency sirens filled the air and relief filled her chest. Someone must have seen the smoke and called the fire department. She prayed the heavy snow would keep the fire from spreading while the firefighters did their work.

Benjamin carried her through the trees, up toward the house, holding her to his chest. She lay her head on his shoulder, safe in his arms.

Lost in her thoughts she noticed the sirens had stopped. Another sound took over the air.

Voices singing.

"The thrill of hope. The weary world rejoices."

It was as if an entire choir was singing carols.

"Can you hear that?"

"Yeah." His head shook in wonder "It's unreal."

"For yonder breaks a new and glorious morn..."

They followed the sound up the hill. Once they'd passed the tree line they saw the top of The Downs. The roof had caved, the turrets had fallen. But every nook and cranny of the building was covered in shimmering ice, as water blasted from the firefighters' hoses. A frozen castle, it was the most beautiful, surreal sight she'd ever seen.

One of the firefighters ran toward them. "Let me take her."

Benjamin held her close. "No, we're good. Just point me to the paramedics."

He directed them around the front of the house.

"Did you manage to pull anyone else from the house?" Piper asked.

The firefighter nodded. "Three men. They're on their way to the hospital now."

"Please mention to the paramedics that the overweight, middle-aged gentleman seems to be suffering from some kind of mental breakdown," Benjamin said. "He's violent but he's not in his right mind and seems to be trapped in the past."

They kept walking. Piper leaned her head into the crook of Benjamin's neck.

"I know he hurt you terribly and murdered Charlotte," he said, "but Tobias is still a very sick man. I hope the justice he faces is still mingled with some mercy."

Piper kissed his cheek. "I know, and I adore that about you."

Lord, have mercy on them all.

They walked around the front of the house. Then she

saw the carolers. Dozens of them were milling about in The Downs parking lot behind the emergency vehicles and police tape, singing carols and holding candles. They poured mugs of hot cocoa and coffee, and passed around muffins as they linked arms. Praying. Singing. Watching. Waiting.

The sun had risen on Christmas morning. And the community had brought Christmas to The Downs.

"It's Piper!" One voice rose from the crowd. "Thank You, Lord!"

"Aunt Cass!"

Her aunt was sitting in a folding chair behind the line of police tape, beside the ambulances, Harry cuddled at her feet and Uncle Des by her side. Benjamin ran toward them. He dropped gently down to one knee beside Aunt Cass, holding Piper to his chest, and she felt her aunt's and uncle's arms slide around her.

"You're hurt," her uncle said.

"Nothing serious. A bullet grazed me. But Benjamin bound it. I'll be okay." She glanced back at the shimmering pile of wood that was once her aunt and uncle's home. "I'm just sorry we couldn't save The Downs."

"Sir." Benjamin was by Uncle Des's side. "I have a boat. It's not much. But if I can find a buyer for it, it might be enough to help give you a head start to getting back on your feet."

Piper's hands grabbed his. "No, Benjamin. Don't. That boat is your dream. You've been saving for it your entire life. You can't give it up for me. I won't let you."

His finger ran down along the side of her face and curled under the back of her neck. "But I love you and I don't want you to lose your home."

"I love you, too," Piper said, "and I don't want you to lose your boat."

Uncle Des smiled. "Thank you for the offer, Benjamin. But whatever we do with The Downs now, it won't involve robbing anyone of their dreams."

Then the old man's eyes turned to Piper. "Your aunt and I had a very long talk last night after you left, mostly about our own dreams and the promises we made to each other. Your aunt Cass gave up her home in England to follow me here. I think it's about time I make good on my promise to take her back home. We don't know what shape that's going to take, but now that The Downs is gone it really feels like the dream we thought we were chasing here isn't going to happen. We'll take a hard look at our finances, see what happens with insurance, contact some of your aunt's friends and family, and try to move back. Now, before you argue, there are good doctors and hospitals in England, too, just like there are here, plus there's less snow to get around so that will help."

Aunt Cass and Uncle Des were going to move across the ocean at their age? With their health problems?

But any doubt Piper had in her mind was quelled when she saw her uncle take her aunt's hand and watched the joy dance in their eyes. The elderly couple bent toward each other in a kiss like the one they'd shared thousands of times before.

Benjamin picked Piper back up in his arms again and started carrying her toward the paramedics, Harry trotting along by his side. Benjamin's mouth brushed over her hair. "I want our love to be like theirs."

So do I.

"But wait." She squeezed his arm. Benjamin stopped.

"If my uncle and aunt move to southern England, I'm going with them. There's nothing keeping me here in Canada. It'll be a huge adventure for them." An exciting once actually. She'd finally be able to see the country where she'd been born. "But they're still going to need my help. If they move, I'm going, too."

"I know." He bent his head toward hers until their foreheads touched. "Fortunately, pet laws being what they are, you should be able to take Harry with you no problem. I'm sure he'll learn to bark with a British accent in no time."

"But what about us?" She closed her eyes and breathed him in. "England isn't Canada, but it's still not Australia."

"Nope, it's not." Benjamin laughed. "It's a whole lot colder and lot farther north. I don't know right this very second how we're going to make this work. But I know with my whole heart that I want to. Now that I know I love you and that you love me, I promise I will do whatever it takes to find a way for us to have a chance at spending our lives together. That's all I have to give you this Christmas—the promise that no matter what, I will find a way."

"That's the best Christmas gift you could give me."

Light snow fell down around them and carols filled the air as Piper brought her lips up to his.

"Merry Christmas, Piper."

"Merry Christmas, Benjamin," she whispered back.

EPILOGUE

A late-August sunrise danced on the dark gray water of the English Channel. Piper's footsteps picked slowly over the smooth stones of the shoreline. A light chill brushed off the early-morning waters. Still, she kicked her sandals off and ran barefoot down the marina's maze of docks. Harry's paws thudded down the wood behind her. She reached the end of an empty slip and sat. Her legs hung over the edge, her feet brushing just above the gentle waves. Her eyes stared out over the expanse of water to the hazy outline of France on the opposite shores. She slipped her phone out of her pocket and turned it on.

For someone who'd never been a fan of getting up early in the morning, it was funny how quickly this had become her favorite time of day. As Benjamin's global sailing trip had him crossing time zones, several hours ahead of her, they'd agreed that whenever he was able to find a phone he'd call her at six o'clock in the morning her time.

Harry stretched out on the dock beside her. Golden rays of sunlight danced along the water. The clock passed six. Her phone didn't ring. She sighed. It had been nine days since Benjamin had been able to make the phone call. Six days since he'd even sent an email.

She opened the email program on her phone to write to him. But instead her eyes ran over the list of emails they'd exchanged in the almost eight months since they'd said goodbye. Her emails had all been so long and chatty, full of news about the sale of the remains of The Downs to a historical society, the ups and downs of her aunt's health journey, the criminal charges filed against Tobias, Gavin, Trisha and Cody Aliston, aka "Kodiak," reconciling her friendship with Dominic as he recovered in the hospital, and finally the huge, exciting adventure of helping her uncle and aunt move overseas to start their new lives.

A sailboat shimmered on the horizon, cutting between her and the rising sun. Her fingers scrolled through screen after screen of the words she'd poured out over the months to Benjamin. Her chest ached.

Yes, she knew he'd never been much of a letter writer. He wasn't much for talking on the phone, either. But while his trip around the world might be bringing him closer to England, these past few months had felt as if he was drifting further and further away.

The boat on the horizon grew closer until she could make out the logo on the sails. It was nothing but a small blue-and-white daytrip boat from a boating tour company down the shore in Brighton. They'd better not be heading for the small marina; they'd have a hard time finding a free place to dock.

Her eyes rose to the sky as it lightened above her.

Lord, was I wrong to think that Benjamin and I could have a future together? I trust his heart. I believe in him. And yet, it's been eight months since The Downs burned down and we're no closer to being together.

Voices were shouting back and forth on the boat. The small craft grew closer. Harry leaped to his feet and barked.

"Shush!" She stood, grabbed his collar with one hand and steered them both down the dock. But the dog braced his legs and stood his ground. She pulled a leash from her pocket and clipped it onto his collar. "Come on. Time for breakfast."

"Piper!"

Her name echoed behind her on the morning air. She turned. A strong figure stood tall in the boat, waving his arms above his head.

She dropped the leash.

He dove off the boat. Strong arms cut swiftly through the water toward her. As he came closer, morning rays of sunlight fell on the full wet beard, dazzling smile and eyes that shone even brighter than the first light of morning.

"Benjamin!" Joy filled her chest, filling her eyes with tears and her mouth with laughter.

He reached her. Two strong hands gripped the dock and then he pulled himself up onto it and stood in front of her, water streaming down his body. She threw her arms around him, anyway. Felt his strong arms pull her tight toward her. Tilted her face toward him and let his mouth find hers in the kiss her heart had ached to feel for eight long months. Then he pulled back and she felt the warmth of his gaze on her face.

"What are you doing here? Where's your boat?"

"I landed in Brighton late last night. My boat's docked there. I'm sorry for not calling, but I didn't want to wake you. A friend of mine gave me a ride over this morning. He's also agreed to give me a job." His hand brushed over the back of her hair. "I'm sorry, baby. I got you soaked."

"I'll dry." She laughed. "You're the one who jumped off a boat."

"I couldn't see a place to dock and this couldn't wait a second longer." He reached into his pocket and pulled out a small waterproof container, the kind boaters kept their valuables in. The clear plastic box seemed to glitter in his hands like a block of ice. Her heart leaped in her chest.

He knelt on the dock in front of her, as a slender band of diamonds and gold tumbled out into his palm. "When we said goodbye at Christmas, I promised I'd find a way to spend my life with you. And I've missed you every day, with every breath since then. I thought I'd just finish my voyage first, and that all this could wait until I'd made it once around the world. But I can't wait any longer. There's no adventure worth having without you beside me. So, I'm dropping anchor. Here. Now. With you."

But she grabbed his outstretched hand with both of hers before a marriage proposal could pass his lips. Her knees dropped down to the wood until they were kneeling face-to-face. "Wait. What about your boat, your life, your dream?"

"I'll run short boating trips around the British Isles and France. Then, whenever you're ready—no matter how many years it takes—we'll lift anchor, and you and I can sail the world together." The smooth circle of the engagement ring pressed into the skin between their palms. "You are worth waiting for."

Her lips trembled. But she forced them still and took a deep breath.

Everything inside her was bursting to say yes to the question he had yet to ask. Her heart ached to just fall deep into his arms and to stay there forever. Yes, her uncle and aunt were in a better place now, living with a cousin of her aunt's who was a retired nurse. With no business to run, they didn't need her living with them full-time and could probably even go without her for a couple of days at a time.

But still. Was he sure?

Was she?

They'd had so many months apart and too many goodbyes already. Could she trust that this time he'd stay?

"My aunt still doesn't have a firm diagnosis," she said. "They're renting a place from family. I'm just working part-time. I don't know how long you'd need to stay anchored for. Are you sure you want to risk your whole future on me?"

"My beloved." Benjamin brushed her hair from her face. "I took the biggest risk of my life when I walked across the store floor to talk to you a year ago, because I knew the moment our eyes met that my heart was going to fall into your hands." He pulled the ring out from between their clasped hands. "Please, marry me, Piper. Be my best friend and my partner in this life. Share all my adventures with me and I'll share yours with you. No matter what the future brings."

A question echoed deep and sincere in the blue of his eyes, aching for an answer.

A look she knew she could trust.

Peace filled her heart. "Yes. Of course I will. Yes!"

He slid the ring on her finger. Her arms flew around his neck, so fast it sent her glasses tumbling off her face and clattering onto the dock. She closed her eyes as his lips found hers again. And the light of the morning sun brushed over them, filling their bodies with warmth.

* * * * *

Dear Reader,

What's the hardest Christmas you've ever had? For me, it was the year I moved from the south of England back home to Canada with a toddler and newborn infant. I'll never forget the chaos at the airport, with people lined up outside to get in, a crying baby in my arms and the fear that I wouldn't make my flight. Thankfully, I had a supportive man to share the load and we all arrived safe and sound on the other side of the ocean where my wonderful in-laws took us in while we looked for a home. That Christmas Eve, my life truly felt like a car spinning out of control on the ice. It helped me learn that sometimes, despite all your best planning and intentions, chaos happens and all you can do is hold on, hold together and pray while you wait for the storm to pass.

Thank you so much for reading this book! I was so excited to bring Benjamin back for a story of his own, after he and Harry the dog appeared as part of Meg's story in *Deadline* (August 2014), as well as to introduce you to Piper. She was such a fun, spunky and caring character to write. If you want to get in touch please visit me at www.maggiekblack.com or follow me @maggiekblack on Twitter.

Wishing you a wonderful Christmas season whatever the holidays bring this year.

Thank you for sharing the journey,

Maggie

REQUEST YOUR FREE BOOKS!

2 FREE RIVETING INSPIRATIONAL NOVELS
PLUS 2 FREE MYSTERY GIFTS

Love Inspired®
SUSPENSE
RIVETING INSPIRATIONAL ROMANCE

YES! Please send me 2 FREE Love Inspired® Suspense novels and my 2 FREE mystery gifts (gifts are worth about $10). After receiving them, if I don't wish to receive any more books, I can return the shipping statement marked "cancel." If I don't cancel, I will receive 4 brand-new novels every month and be billed just $4.99 per book in the U.S. or $5.49 per book in Canada. That's a savings of at least 17% off the cover price. It's quite a bargain! Shipping and handling is just 50¢ per book in the U.S. and 75¢ per book in Canada.* I understand that accepting the 2 free books and gifts places me under no obligation to buy anything. I can always return a shipment and cancel at any time. Even if I never buy another book, the two free books and gifts are mine to keep forever.

123/323 IDN GH5Z

Name _____ (PLEASE PRINT) _____

Address _____ Apt. #

City _____ State/Prov. _____ Zip/Postal Code

Signature (if under 18, a parent or guardian must sign)

Mail to the **Reader Service:**
IN U.S.A.: P.O. Box 1867, Buffalo, NY 14240-1867
IN CANADA: P.O. Box 609, Fort Erie, Ontario L2A 5X3

**Are you a current subscriber to Love Inspired® Suspense books
and want to receive the larger-print edition?
Call 1-800-873-8635 or visit www.ReaderService.com.**

* Terms and prices subject to change without notice. Prices do not include applicable taxes. Sales tax applicable in N.Y. Canadian residents will be charged applicable taxes. Offer not valid in Quebec. This offer is limited to one order per household. Not valid for current subscribers to Love Inspired Suspense books. All orders subject to credit approval. Credit or debit balances in a customer's account(s) may be offset by any other outstanding balance owed by or to the customer. Please allow 4 to 6 weeks for delivery. Offer available while quantities last.

Your Privacy—The Reader Service is committed to protecting your privacy. Our Privacy Policy is available online at www.ReaderService.com or upon request from the Reader Service.
We make a portion of our mailing list available to reputable third parties that offer products we believe may interest you. If you prefer that we not exchange your name with third parties, or if you wish to clarify or modify your communication preferences, please visit us at www.ReaderService.com/consumerschoice or write to us at Reader Service Preference Service, P.O. Box 9062, Buffalo, NY 14240-9062. Include your complete name and address.

LIS15

SPECIAL EXCERPT FROM

Love Inspired
SUSPENSE

*When new evidence surfaces that Harper Shelby's niece
is alive, Harper doesn't expect it to endanger her life.
But Logan Fitzgerald is there to save the day and help
her uncover the truth.*

Read on for a sneak preview of
DEADLY CHRISTMAS SECRETS by
Shirlee McCoy,
*available in December 2015
from Love Inspired Suspense!*

Logan Fitzgerald had a split second to realize he'd been used before the first bullet flew. He didn't like it. Didn't like that he'd been used to find a woman whom someone apparently wanted dead.

Gabe Wilson?

Probably, but Logan didn't have time to think about it. Not now. Later he'd figure things out.

For now, he just had to stay alive, keep Harper alive.

He pulled his handgun, fired a shot into the front windshield of the dark sedan. Not a kill shot, but it was enough to take out the glass, cause a distraction.

He shoved Harper toward the tree line. "Go!" he shouted, firing another shot, this one in the front tire.

She scrambled into the bushes, her giant dog following along behind her.

The sedan backed up, tires squealing as the driver tried to speed away. Not an easy task with a flat tire, and Logan caught a glimpse of two men. One dark-haired. One bald. He fired toward the gunman and saw the bald guy duck as the bullet slammed into what remained of the windshield.

He could have pursued them, shot out another tire, tried to take them both down. This was what he was trained to do—face down the opponent, win. But Harper had run into the woods. He didn't know how far, didn't know if she was out of range of the gunman or close enough to take a stray bullet.

He knew what he wanted to do—pursue the gunman, find out who had hired him, find out why.

He also knew what his boss, Chance Miller, would say—protect the innocent first. Worry about the criminals later.

He'd have been right.

Logan knew it, but he still wanted to hunt the gunmen down.

He holstered his gun and stepped into the trees, the sound of the car thumping along the gravel road ringing through the early morning.

He moved down a steep embankment, following a trail of footprints in the damp earth. He could hear a creek babbling, the quiet melody belying the violence that had just occurred.

The car engine died, the thump of tires ceasing.

A door opened. Closed.

Was the gunman pursuing them?

He lost the trail of footprints at a creek that tripped along the base of a deep embankment.

He wanted to call to Harper, draw her out of her hiding place, but the forest had gone dead silent.

He moved cautiously, keeping low as he crossed the creek and searched for footprints in the mucky earth. The scent of dead leaves filled his nose, the late November air slicing through his jacket. He ignored the cold. Ignored everything but his mission—finding Harper Shelby and keeping her alive.

Don't miss
DEADLY CHRISTMAS SECRETS
by Shirlee McCoy, available December 2015 wherever
Love Inspired® Suspense books and ebooks are sold.

"Everything has changed, hasn't it?"

Finn heard the same catch in her tone that he felt in his own chest. He knew he was Finn Brannigan, but didn't know if that was good news. The sense that the life he'd forgotten wasn't a happy one still pressed against him.

"So it's just your name? That's all you remember?"

"And my age." *Tell her you're a Ranger*, the honorable side of him scolded the other part that foolishly refused to confess. It felt as though everything would slam back into place once tomorrow dawned, so would it be terrible to just keep this one night as the happy victory it was? She'd be perfectly entitled to refuse his friendship once all the facts came to light.

Amelia laid her hand on his arm and he felt that connection he had each time she touched him. As if she needed him, even though it was the other way around. "I can't imagine what you must be feeling right now."

The return of his memory was a double-edged sword. "There's a lot floating out there—fuzzy impressions I can't quite get a fix on, but…I can't tell you what it means to know my whole name." He hesitated for a moment before admitting, "For a while I was terrified it wouldn't come back. That I'd end up one of those freak stories you read about in supermarket tabloids."

She laughed. "I can't imagine that. You're far too normal."

Normal? Nothing about him felt normal. The scary part was the constant sense that his normal wasn't anywhere near as nice as right now was, sitting out under the stars near a roaring fire hearing…

Christmas carols. A group of high school students began to sing "Away in a Manger." Finn felt his stomach tighten.

He waited for his unnamed aversion to all things Christmas to wash over him. It came, but more softly. More like regret than flat-out hate. Finn closed his eyes and tried to hear it the way Amelia did, reverent and quiet instead of slow and mournful. Why couldn't he grasp the big dark thing lurking just out of his reach? What made him react to Christmas the way he did?

Don't miss
A RANGER FOR THE HOLIDAYS
by Allie Pleiter, available December 2015 wherever
Love Inspired® books and ebooks are sold.